Sit, Stay, Love

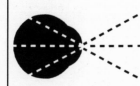

This Large Print Book carries the
Seal of Approval of N.A.V.H.

SIT, STAY, LOVE

DANA MENTINK

THORNDIKE PRESS

A part of Gale, Cengage Learning

Farmington Hills, Mich • San Francisco • New York • Waterville, Maine
Meriden, Conn • Mason, Ohio • Chicago

GALE
CENGAGE Learning®

LIBRARY OF CONGRESS CATALOGING-IN-PUBLICATION DATA

Names: Mentink, Dana, author.
Title: Sit, stay, love / by Dana Mentink.
Description: Large print edition. | Waterville, Maine : Thorndike Press, 2016. |
  © 2016 | Series: Thorndike Press large print Christian romance
Identifiers: LCCN 2016009895| ISBN 9781410490469 (hardcover) | ISBN 1410490467
  (hardcover)
Subjects: LCSH: Large type books.
Classification: LCC PS3613.E496 S55 2016b | DDC 813/.6—dc23
LC record available at http://lccn.loc.gov/2016009895

Published in 2016 by arrangement with Harvest House

Printed in Mexico
1 2 3 4 5 6 7 20 19 18 17 16

To Pat Williams
who graciously shared his love for
baseball and his passion for God.

Dogs are better than human beings
because they know but do not tell.

EMILY DICKINSON

How can you believe since you accept
glory from one another but do not seek
the glory that comes from the only God?

JOHN 5:44

The author would like to thank a special group of volunteers who care for our canine senior citizens. The folks at Muttville make it their mission to rescue elderly dogs from shelters, find loving homes for those dogs that are adoptable, and tenderly care for those who are not. It takes a full measure of compassion to show such love and tireless dedication to God's noblest and most unselfish creatures. Thank you, Muttville, for reminding us that it is never too late for love. Tippy and I salute you!

ONE

"What is that?" Cal Crawford looked in disgust from Pete to the sagging bundle under his pitching coach's arm.

"It's a dog, of course," Pete said. "Your mother's dog. What kind of a question is that?"

The dog stared at Cal with mournful brown eyes. Or maybe it was the hang-down ears or the graying jowls that added to the gloom on the gaze. "I've had dogs. Hunting dogs. That's not in the same line."

"She's a dog all right, a dachshund mixed with something taller and wider." Pete gave the animal a conciliatory rub between the eyebrows. "I've been taking care of her since the funeral."

Cal shifted. He'd forgotten. He'd been on the road when his mother passed away and Pete had taken care of the details, Cal flying in just before the funeral and jetting off immediately after. "That's right," he said. "It

9

was good of you to do that, Pete."

"Yeah, it was, but I've got to have my boat rehauled and anyway Tippy's not a good sailor. I think she's prone to seasickness."

Cal winced as the physical therapist kneaded the sore muscle in his shoulder. Shouldn't be so tender, not in the off-season. He shoved the thought aside. The dog stared at him. "So why did you bring it here?"

"Her, not it. Name's Tippy, like I said, and your mother wouldn't want her to go to the pound. I've asked everyone from the short-stop to the hot dog vendors and no one wants a thirteen-year-old mutt of dubious ancestry."

Cal gaped as the facts assembled themselves in his mind. "You're not thinking that I'm going to take it?"

"Why not?"

"Spring training's coming up."

Pete quirked a sarcastic eyebrow. "I'm aware. We work for the same team, you know."

"I'm a starter."

"I'm aware of that, too, Mr. Big Shot Pitcher. I've been watching you since single A ball, sonny boy, when you couldn't lace your cleats by yourself, so don't put on airs with me."

Cal was adrift at what Pete seemed to be asking him to do. "I don't like dogs that don't work for their keep."

"You make a seven-figure salary. Hire someone to like her for you." Pete placed the ungainly dog on the floor and gave her a scratch behind the ears. Her knobby paws slowly slid outward on the slick flooring until she oozed like a puddle, round belly first, onto the tile. "Here's your new daddy, Tippy. He's kind of crabby for such a young guy, but don't let that fool you. He's still grieving for his mama. Underneath, he's got a heart of gold." Pete shot Cal a look. "Somewhere."

Cal leapt out of the massage chair. "You can't leave me with this animal."

Pete fished a tattered rectangle from his pocket. "Here's a card for a dog sitter."

"But . . ."

"She's vetted and trained; she works with celebrity clients exclusively. Takes care of Coach Bruce's goldens when the missus is out of town."

"I can't . . ."

"Yes, you can. I've got a meeting. See you later."

Cal clutched the card. "No, Pete. This is not happening. I am not taking this dog."

"She eats pretty much anything and she's

11

already had breakfast," he said.

"I'm not doing this."

Pete headed down the hallway. "And whatever you do, don't let her near your car keys."

"Why?" Cal yelled down the corridor. "What does it do with car keys?"

"She," Pete thundered. "Tippy's a girl."

Gina sat in her cousin's car, fingers clenched on the wheel, staring at the gate which separated her from a house she would never be able to afford in six lifetimes. Maybe seven. Sea Cliff, San Francisco, was not the natural habitat of a girl of Gina's financial circumstances. Her hand hovered over the gear, eager to slam the Volvo into reverse and flee. *God will equip you for anything, remember?* Her insides quivered as she recalled that she hadn't exactly made a spectacular success out of her last endeavor. She whispered another prayer, hoping the equipping would commence immediately, in great quantity, and inched the car up to the guard whose nametag identified him as Ed. She smiled, he smiled, and she admired the little crayon sketch taped on the wall next to his phone with a name scrawled in crooked capital letters underneath. Addie Jo. The guard's granddaughter, he told her with a proud smile. They chatted about Addie Jo, the artistic four-year-old who was learning ballet and had a bowl full of guppies that would not stop reproducing.

After looking her over and consulting a clipboard, miraculously, he let her pass. Maybe it really had been a good idea to put on the blue blazer and skirt, though it seemed pretty ridiculous for pet-sitter garb. She'd never met a dog who seemed at all impressed by stylish clothing.

"These are celebrity clients," her cousin Lexi had said. "Humor them; treat them with kid gloves."

Gina would rather be at school with her kindergartners, wrist-deep in finger paints, fat pencils, and safety scissors, than trying to impress celebrities. *They aren't your kindergartners anymore, remember?* Pain pricked at her heart. She'd served her three months as a long-term sub, long enough to fall in love with the ornery, boisterous five-year-olds. There might have even been a full-time position in the works if she hadn't accidentally misplaced a child during the class field trip to the bakery. One minute she had twenty-six students, and the next, Rodney Wang was missing, only to be discovered sleeping atop a massive stack of flour an hour and a half later after a frantic search that included the police. The end of her dream.

Goodbye, Teacher Palmer. Hello unemployment, which had lasted five interminable weeks until her cousin had to deal with the hernia that would not be ignored. Goodbye, kindergarten. Hello, celebrity pet concierge. *Don't worry, cuz. I won't mess things up.* She intended to prove herself this time, like she'd been trying to do since the moment of her birth, it seemed. She read her notes again. Cal Crawford. Cal like California and Crawford like . . . Joan? Just a helpful little memory game, like those she'd used to stagger through college algebra.

Parking on the wide sweep of drive, she was admitted past a breathtaking marble foyer and into an even fancier living room by a man in a suit. The color palette of blues and grays was soothing, the perfect backdrop to the sleek furniture.

"Mr. Crawford will be here in a moment," said the man in the suit.

Before she could strike up a conversation, he excused himself with a, "Please make yourself at home."

Home? Her home was a rented room above a pierogi shop with an old fruit crate serving as a coffee table and a view of a parking lot. This place was all shining wood floors, rich oil paintings, and manly leather furniture. Should she sit? No, too familiar. She stayed standing, hands in her pockets. No, that wasn't professional. She tried clasping them behind her back. Too schoolgirl. Folding her arms across her chest? Confrontational. She was just going for one hand on her hip and the other resting on the pristine oak sideboard when a dog skidded into the room, nails scrabbling for purchase on the wood floor.

She was clearly an old dog, her coat a soft butterscotch color and her muzzle graying. Two droopy ears framed a set of eyes filmed with cataracts, mournful and expectant at the same time. The animal slipped and slid, finally coming to a stop at Gina's feet.

Forgetting her professional demeanor, Gina dropped to her knees and caressed the dog. "Aren't you a sweetie?" she crooned in baby talk. It was something that happened every time she spoke to a dog. Her vocabulary regressed some twenty-seven years, much to her cousin's dismay. "What's the matter, little pumpkin pie? Is this horrible floor too slippery for you?"

"The horrible floor happens to be mahogany, and its nails are leaving scratches."

She leapt to her feet so fast her head spun,

finding herself face to face with a man a good six inches taller. He was lean and muscular with a stubble of brown on his tanned chin, chocolate eyes regarding her from under thick brows. Handsome, but handsome was way overrated, as she'd recently learned.

She pulled up his last name from her ragged short-term memory files. Crawford like Joan. "You must be Mr. Crawford."

"Cal, and you are Lexi?" He eyed her skeptically. A lazy drawl added unexpected softness to the words.

The moment of truth. *Time to sell it, Gina.* "Actually, I'm her cousin Gina. Lexi had to have some minor surgery done, so I'm filling in."

One brow wriggled upward. "And you're a dog expert?"

She tugged on her jacket. "Of course. Don't I look like one?"

His mouth quirked. "I guess. You just sounded funny when you were talking to it."

"You mean the dog?" She hoped her cheeks weren't too badly flushed, but there was no hope, really. A strawberry blonde with skin a shade lighter than a fish belly ensured that the slightest embarrassment lit up her face like a neon sign. Always had.

She went for dignified. "I was informed the dog is a female, Mr. Crawford. Is that correct?"

"You can call me Cal. Yeah. Name's Tippy."

They both looked at the sprawled creature that had flopped over on her side, stubby legs twitching.

"She wants a tummy scratch," Gina said.

Cal looked at her like she was suggesting he swallow a live toad.

"Like this," she said. Kneeling again, she scratched Tippy's stomach. The dog let out a snuffle of pure contentment and closed her eyes. "See?"

Cal shifted. "Listen, Gina. I have to make something clear. I'm busy. I'm a pitcher for the Falcons and we're just heading into spring training."

She kept on scratching and looked up at Cal. "Uh huh."

"It's a rigorous schedule. Conditioning, strategy work, studying film, lots of press time."

She resisted an eye roll. *If you think playing a game is rigorous, try teaching kindergarten.*

"And I'm on the road a lot. When the season starts, I'm traveling all the time."

Yep, hard life. Four-star hotels. Private planes. Catered meals. Gina tried to recall what she'd had for breakfast. A two-day-old egg roll.

"Are you listening to me?" Cal demanded.

Lexi's admonishment resurfaced. Kid gloves. She stood. Tippy cracked an eyelid but did not move.

"Yes, Mr. Crawford. On the road. Traveling. Rigorous. I was listening."

He shoved his hands in the pockets of his expensive jeans which, she noticed, fit him extremely well.

"Anyway, I don't have the time to care for it."

"Her."

"Yes, her," he snapped. "I want you to take her."

"Take her?"

"Can you do that?" A sheen of hope washed over his face. "Take Tippy to live at your house? I'd pay whatever you want."

"I'm sorry, but my landlady doesn't allow dogs."

His mouth tightened. "I'll rent you another place. A house, or a condo. One that takes pets. I'll pay for it all. And living expenses."

She gaped. Blood rushed to her cheeks, no doubt broadcasting her emotions, notably the anger that fizzed up in her belly. "Listen, Mr. Crawford. I realize you're a

18

big shot athlete and all that, but I'm not some desperate girl who's going to let men rent living spaces and pay my expenses. I'm a pet sitter. That's it, and you can find yourself another one, by the way." She stalked to the door. Not waiting for the suited man to appear and open it, she wrenched the handle herself.

"Wait," Cal called, stepping over the still sprawled dog. "Wait, I . . . I apologize. I didn't meant to insult you. I'm just sort of desperate."

She turned, searching for sincerity in his expression and finding a gleam that might qualify, but her man judgment was not the greatest, as recent history bore out. "Why do you own this dog when you clearly don't want her?"

He paused. "Inheritance."

"From whom?"

He looked down, suddenly morphing into a little boy. "My mom."

His mother. Lexi told her his mother had passed away of cancer some six months before, but she'd forgotten. "I'm sorry."

He rubbed a hand over his face, which she now noticed was lined with fatigue. "She loved the dog. Told me all kinds of stuff about it."

Stuff? Cal clearly had not spent much

19

time with his mother, yet for some reason he was making an effort to hold onto her beloved dog. Minimal effort, but it was a point in his favor. A very small one. Gina allowed herself to relax a tiny bit. She removed the list from her pocket and reviewed. "I'm happy to help you care for Tippy according to the terms of the contract you signed with my cousin. Grooming and feeding, vet care when needed, a daily walk schedule, and training where appropriate."

"You wrote that all down?"

"It helps me remember. If you want something else, you'll have to hire a different service." She held her breath. With her cousin laid up and her other employee scrambling to cover their current jobs, this one would be Gina's alone until Lexi recovered.

"Okay."

"Okay?"

"Okay. When can you start?"

She tried to hide her grin. "Right now. I've got a leash in the car."

"Fine," he said, exhaling in relief. "That's great."

Gina checked her watch. "When was the last time she ate?"

"Dunno. Think the cook gave her some oatmeal for breakfast."

"Oatmeal? You don't have dog food?"

He shrugged helplessly. "I didn't know I was getting a dog until yesterday. We just gave our working dogs whatever meat was leftover from meals."

"All right. If it's okay to take Tippy for a drive, we'll go by the pet store and pick up some supplies."

"Take her anywhere you want." After a relieved exhale, Cal patted his pockets. "Oh, sorry. My wallet is upstairs. I'll be right back."

"Never mind," Gina said. "I'll bill you."

He nodded. They both looked at Tippy who had not moved, short legs still frozen in the air.

"How long can she stay like that?"

Gina laughed. "Until someone scratches her tummy again."

"Huh." Cal did not laugh as he said goodbye and headed toward the back of the house, but his grimace was not quite as bad, she thought. And why wouldn't he be more cheerful? He'd just offloaded the well-being of his mother's beloved pet to a stranger. Tippy's sad gaze followed Cal as he left the room.

"Well, Tippy," she whispered to the prostrate dog. "Your owner has a real chip on his shoulder, doesn't he? How are you feel-

21

ing about your new digs?"

Tippy let out an enormous sigh that ruffled the soft lips of her graying muzzle.

"My sentiments exactly."

TWO

Cal wandered the house. Not a wanderer by nature, he could not understand why it was now five o'clock on a Monday morning and he had not slept more than three hours the previous night. Again. Much as he'd like to blame it on the snoring of a certain overweight canine who'd somehow burgled her way into the bedroom and crashed in the middle of the plush carpet, the insomnia had started earlier, some six months before.

The sports psychologists they'd had him work with tried to connect it to his mother's illness and death. It wasn't true. She was gone. Yes. He was alone. Definitely, but he'd always been able to will his body to do anything he wanted, from running a six-minute mile to pitching a perfect game to splitting a cord of wood before sunup. With enough hard work, his body obeyed his mind and his mother's death couldn't change that. Nothing could.

So why was he awake?

He considered suiting up for a quick run before his morning appointment. Then again, he should probably eat something since he hadn't been hungry the night before, much to the dismay of Luz, his chef.

On the fridge he found a note from her in all caps. "Junior, I will be here at seven promptly to make you a proper breakfast which you will eat. Luz."

He smiled. Since he'd made it big in pro baseball, people didn't order him around. It was all "Mr. Crawford" and "sir" — except from his teammates, who'd called him "Boots" since he'd shown up to training one unfortunate day still in his ranch clothes. Certainly nobody but his sixty-year-old Hungarian cook called him Junior. He would not admit it under pain of death, but it pleased him.

A clatter of toenails on the hardwood announced Tippy's presence. The dog waddled in and sat, staring up at Cal.

"What?"

The dog stared.

"You hungry?"

More staring. Did it ever blink? The border collies he'd had at the ranch were always on the move. They never sat still, let alone stared at him. Creepy.

"Gotta go outside?" The thought horrified him as he considered the perfectly mani-cured lawns which cost him a cool twenty thousand a year to maintain. But if the dog had to go, better the grass than the Persian rug.

He opened the sliding door. Tippy did not move.

Cal ran a hand over his stubbled chin. "Look, dog. I got things to do today. If you need something, get it from Gina when she comes."

Where was the girl anyway?

As if on cue, the front door opened and Tippy did an awkward three-point turn, trotting off to check out the new arrival. Cal heard a soft burble of baby talk.

The dog sitter had arrived. A sitter for a dog. Ridiculous.

He decided to stay in the kitchen and leave the two to "fellowship," as his mother would have said. The thought stung. He retrieved a bottle of water from the fridge and paced while he drank it.

Gina swept into the kitchen holding a pink box of doughnuts and munching on a sprinkled one. She'd left the starched look at home, this time dressed in a flowered skirt and soft sweater, a gauzy scarf to ward off the February chill. Flowers suited her

25

way more than the blazer. She looked . . . soft, and fresh, and her hair shone as though it might smell like fruity shampoo if he put his nose to it. A far cry from the few girls he'd dated when he first made it to the big leagues, all designer shoes and fancy handbags, the kind that looked natural in the passenger seat of his Porsche but would never have been able to leap up into the front seat of his real car, a Chevy truck. He wondered what type of car Gina drove, then wondered why he was wondering about it.

He drank some more water.

"Good morning, Mr. Crawford. Do you want a doughnut?" she said. "I thought I'd bring some along and introduce myself to your people."

"My people?"

"Sure. The cook and the gardener and such. I already met the security guard and your door guy."

"My door guy?" Why was he repeating everything she said? "Roberto."

"He prefers Bobby. He needed a doughnut, poor guy."

"Why?"

"He's getting divorced from Linda. It's not easy to break apart two lives after sixteen years." She slid the box onto the counter. "You want a sprinkle doughnut? I saved one."

"No."

Her eyes swiveled to the note on the fridge. "Oh, right." She giggled. "I don't want you to get in trouble with your cook for ruining your meal."

He felt a burn of embarrassment. "I don't eat doughnuts because they're basically fat bombs."

She stopped. "Well, of course they are. That's why they're good to eat."

A little yellow sprinkle stuck to the curve of her cheek, right above the dimple. The scent of sugar made his mouth water for his mother's deep-dish peach pie. Odd thought, since he hadn't eaten it in over a year.

She bent to caress Tippy. "Did you feed her?"

"Isn't that your job?"

Gina shot him a look.

"I asked her if she was hungry," he hurried to explain. Inane. He was asking questions of dogs now. Had to be the sleep deprivation. "Dog didn't seem like it wanted anything."

"You look tired," Gina said, eyeing Cal. "Didn't you sleep?" She put out a bowl and filled it with brown nuggets.

"I'm fine. Gotta make a call." Cal excused himself to the study. He didn't really have any such phone call to make, but the dog sitter confused him almost as much as the dog, talking as if she'd known him forever, offering doughnuts and teasing him about Luz. And how come she knew all about Roberto and Linda? He hadn't even known Roberto was married, let alone breaking up with his wife. Not something men talked about.

He read his text from Pete. "Nine o'clock, get loose. Couple of pitches and press time." He wondered how fast they could get the press thing done so he could get rid of them and watch more film of his slider, the pitch that was giving him trouble.

"Mr. Crawford?"

He started. Gina stood at his elbow with the yellow sprinkle still stuck to her cheek, but no dimple showing.

"Yes?"

"I need you in the kitchen for a moment."

Her tone was troubled, lips puckered into a frown.

"You do?"

"Yes."

"Why?"

"I think we have a problem."

He couldn't help himself. He reached out a finger and gently brushed the yellow sprinkle from her satin-soft cheek.

Her eyes opened wide in amazement and her hand flew to her face.

"Sorry. It was a sprinkle," he stammered. "Stuck on you."

Color flooded her cheeks now as if someone had airbrushed her with petal pink. "Oh. Well. Thank you. Anyway, I think there's something wrong with Tippy."

There's plenty wrong with Tippy, he thought, but he followed her into the kitchen anyway. Tippy stood next to her uneaten kibble, tail drooping.

"She won't eat. Are you sure you didn't feed her?"

"Not a thing. Maybe it's the kibble you got her."

"Well, I wet it with chicken broth. How could she not like it?"

He shrugged. "I dunno. You're the dog expert. It could stand to skip a few meals, anyway." He bent to examine the floor. "I really think her nails are messing up the wood. Can you get them clipped?"

Tippy launched herself at Cal. Off balance, he sat down hard. Tippy slurped her long tongue over his face, body wriggling as if she was spring-loaded.

"Knock it off," Cal said, shooing her away with his free hand and wiping his cheek with the other.

29

Tippy trotted happily to her food bowl and began to wolf down the kibble.

"Nothing wrong with her stomach now," Cal grumped. He got to his feet.

Tippy immediately stopped eating, staring at Cal with limpid eyes.

Gina's mouth opened in an *O* of surprise. "I think she wants you to sit with her while she eats."

Cal gaped. "You have got to be out of your mind."

"Just try it. Please?"

Reluctantly, he resumed a sitting position.

Tippy once again began to eat.

He rose.

She stopped.

He sank down again.

She ate.

Cal looked up at Gina in complete disbelief.

"Looks like she'll only eat when you're with her," Gina said, biting her lip against a smile.

"Why would that be?" he managed. "I don't even like her."

Gina shrugged, all doe-eyed innocence. "I guess she doesn't know that."

"Ms. Palmer, I'm not going to sit down on the floor next to this dog at chow time."

"I understand, Mr. Crawford. I'm sure

she'll adjust. It's the new place and all. It's not very" — she looked around — "friendly."

"Not supposed to be friendly," he snapped.

"What were you going for then?" She pursed her lips. "Austere? Luxurious? Manly?"

He had an odd sense that she was teasing him and he was not at all sure how to take it. The truth was, he hadn't consulted on one single detail in the monstrous house. He'd needed a home in San Francisco, told his agent as much, and bingo. One whopper of a check later and the deed was done. But it was all top-of-the-line stuff — beveled glass, pendant lighting, and such. She should be impressed, though the old banged-up couch at the ranch was plenty more comfortable than anything in the entire place.

"I'm sure things will improve as Tippy settles in. Pete said she's been getting three meals a day on his boat, so we'll keep to that schedule for a while until we pare down her calories a bit."

"You've been talking to my pitching coach?"

"Well, of course. Pete's been Tippy's

caretaker. Who would know her better than him?"

He shook his head. "Anyway, I've got to go to the ball field. Contact me if anything comes up."

"How?"

He stopped himself from parroting back her maddening question. Grabbing a paper from the drawer, he scrawled his cell number on it. "Don't give it out to anyone," he said sternly.

"Of course not, Mr. Crawford. You can depend on me."

She looked like a cross between a Girl Scout and a fifties movie star, standing there with her flowered skirt, pink lips, and mischievous smile.

"Call me Cal." He grabbed his duffel bag and iPhone and headed for the door.

"What should I tell her?" Gina called.

"Who?"

"Luz. What should I say when she arrives to make you breakfast and you're not here?"

Inwardly he groaned. "You can eat it for me."

"Okey dokey, Mr. Crawford."

He wondered how Gina Palmer, doughnut queen, was going to enjoy a wheatgrass smoothie and egg white omelet for breakfast. Smiling, he closed the door behind him.

Three antacids later and Gina had finally vanquished the wheatgrass heartburn. Though the breakfast tasted like something that was never meant to cross human lips, Gina had learned a wealth of information from the gregarious Luz.

The gray-haired lady, immaculately dressed in slacks and a white silk blouse, referred to Cal as "Mr. Cal," leading Gina to believe that Junior must be a name uttered only in private. She'd been cooking for him since he bought the San Francisco home a year before.

"He works too hard, Mr. Cal. All skin and muscle and not sleeping. Not good for a young boy."

Gina knew Cal was twenty-eight which, in Luz's mind, must be just out of high school. "Why isn't he sleeping?"

Luz shrugged. "Too much pressure. Everyone expects him to be a superstar. And now? No mama to share it with." She looked slyly at Gina. "And no girlfriend either."

Gina coughed. *Don't look at me. I'd never date a dog hater.* "Was he close to his mother?"

Luz clucked. "Ah. I've talked too much. I'm to go to the market and pick up a few

33

things. Some fresh spinach for steaming. That will fix up Mr. Cal."

Gina was still thinking a sprinkle dough- nut would do the cranky pitcher more good than steamed spinach, but she didn't say so. She and Tippy went for a very slow walk in the February sunshine, which came to an abrupt end when Tippy sat down after two blocks and refused to budge. She had to carry her back to Cal's place. Both Tippy and Gina required a nap after the exertion and Tippy woke eager for lunch. Gina poured the kibble, complete with bits of chopped chicken, in a bowl.

Tippy lay down and stared.

Gina sat next to her with no better result.

Nothing would tempt the dog to eat. She thought about calling Cal's cell phone, but she figured he was busy with the throwing and catching thing. Her best chance was to get the dog to him. It would take no more than a minute. Surely he would have time for that.

"Like mom always says, if the mountain won't come to you . . ." She put Tippy's bowl into a bag along with the kibble and drove. The stadium was closed, but she found a security guard named Abe and explained all about Tippy. By the time she'd finished the story about the dog's need for eating companionship from Cal, Abe was laughing until the tears ran down his face.

"I thought I'd heard everything," he chortled.

He agreed to escort Gina to the dugout after she promised not to interfere with the practice.

"We'll wait patiently until Mr. Crawford is finished, I promise."

Still laughing, the guard guided Gina and Tippy to the field. The two of them settled onto a bench with a perfect view of the proceedings. The green of the grass and the enormous sweep of empty red seats floored her. Imagine all those people paying good money to go and stare at some guys trying to hit a ball with a stick. Maybe it was all about the snacks.

She stroked Tippy's ears as she watched.

Pete was there along with several men she had not met. Cal was dressed in his uniform, cap low on his forehead, the number eleven pulled taut across his muscled shoulders. Behind home plate, a catcher crouched to take his pitch, looking like some weird sort of insect with all the padded gear covering him like an exoskeleton. A photographer with an enormous camera stood next to Pete, taking picture after picture. Cal ignored it all, riveted on the ball in his hands

35

and some imaginary bull's-eye in the center of the catcher's mitt.

Gina could only imagine such focus. She could rarely make it through one magazine article without her attention drifting a hundred different directions — a leftover from her traumatic entry into the world, the doctors said, along with the memory problems and a tendency to catch every cold bug that came around.

Cal fired a pitch that went so fast it was nothing more than a blur. She gasped. No wonder the guy kept in such good shape if he had to do that for a living. With such torque on his arm, she did not see how it hadn't snapped off at the elbow. The smack of the pitch into the catcher's mitt echoed through the air.

Tippy shifted in her lap, her nails scratching Gina's legs.

"See, Tippy? This is how Cal spends his time, playing ball, only there's no fetching involved, at least from him."

Another blistering pitch from Cal. The photographer clicked away, crouched down to get the best shot. Cal took off his cap and wiped his forehead with the back of his hand before replacing it.

Suddenly, Tippy made a mysterious canine connection. She stiffened, ears in a semi-upright position, nose twitching, entranced by the goings-on.

"Stay, Tippy," Gina murmured in the dog's ear. "He's working."

The catcher readied the ball to throw it back to Cal.

Tippy launched herself off Gina's lap, yanking the leash free, and took off running for Cal.

"No, Tippy," Gina shouted.

Cal's attention jerked toward Tippy just as the catcher loosed the ball. It sailed through the air and hit him square in the face with a thunk.

Gina clapped her hands over her mouth in horror. Cal's head snapped back. He fell backward onto the pitcher's mound.

THREE

Cal's vision cleared enough that he could see the panic-stricken face of catcher Julio Aguilera looming over him, blotting out the San Francisco sky. He blinked hard, a low ringing in his ears.

Julio was on his knees, mask off, eyebrows raised nearly to his hairline.

"Boots? You alive, man?"

"I think so."

He smiled, then frowned, then grimaced in a way that would have made the bearded bear of a man terrifying if Cal didn't know him better.

"What are you doing, losing your focus? I could have killed you."

"I'm not dead," Cal repeated, as if this was a logical detail to reiterate.

Julio was beyond logic. He stood up and lapsed into a Spanish tirade. "Could have knocked your scrawny head off, Boots."

Julio wasn't exaggerating. If the catcher's

throw had been anything like his "pop time," the time it took him to fire the ball to second base, Cal would probably be fighting for his life or dead on the spot. As it was, that easy throw was still enough to mess him up, as Cal was beginning to experience. Something like pain began to trickle along his nerves and everything about his face seemed thick and slow.

Pete laid a hand on his chest. "Stay there. Medics are coming."

"Don't need a medic," he mumbled.

Did he? Had a momentary lack of concentration caused a skull fracture? A concussion? Or permanent damage that would strip him of his career? In spite of the sensation that he'd taken a two by four to the cheek, Cal forced himself into a sitting position. Sparks danced in his field of vision, Julio and Pete blurring for a moment.

"You never listen," Pete grumbled, but his eyes brimmed with genuine concern. "Wouldja sit still already? You're worse than Tippy."

Tippy. That word sank through the fog in his brain. Cal blinked, reliving the past few moments. He'd been focused, pitching for the benefit of the camera, then *wham*.

With effort, Cal turned his head. Photo guy was still there, but now he was on one knee, snapping pictures as fast as his Nikon would allow. Pete stood to block the shots. "That's enough now. Have some decency. We got an injury here, for criminy's sake," he growled. Pete called to the security guard. "Escort this gentleman out, would ya?"

The guard was standing with a restraining arm on Gina's shoulder as she struggled to hold onto a wriggling Tippy.

Gina. And Tippy.

"Why is that dog here?" he wanted to say. "Did that crazy woman actually bring the thing to the ballpark?" But it was too many syllables, and his nose was now dripping blood into his mouth and on his uniform shirt. Pete handed him a towel, still trying to block the photographer's view.

The guard hustled forward, brow furrowed, and led the photographer away . . . but not until the guy got off one more picture. The blood shot. He'd get paid well for it.

Cal shook his head to clear it, but that only got him a shooting pain in his temple and one in his arm where Pete was squeezing his bicep. "Stay still, Cal. I mean it."

Julio was pacing now, muttering to himself, anguished, sneaking looks.

"Relax, Ag. I'm okay," he said, even

40

though he fought to say it through lips that were swelling right along with his cheek.

Ag continued to mumble and Cal got the gist, if not the words.

What were you thinking, looking away, like some kid in his first Little League game?

What had he been thinking? He tried to recall.

Somehow the team medic arrived with a cart and Pete and Julio helped him onto it. Every movement made his head nearly explode with pain. He groaned and he heard an echoing female cry.

"Oh, Mr. Crawford," Gina said, moving close and hauling Tippy with her. "I'm so sorry. I would never have believed that Tippy would have run for you like that. Actually I didn't think she could run. Walking completely winds her."

She talked on, trying to gesture and hold on to the animal at the same time. "I mean one moment Tippy was right by my side and the next . . . I feel just terrible." She let out another cry as he lowered the towel. "Oh my gosh. Your face. And you're bleeding." She gulped and he thought he saw the gleam of tears in her eyes. Part of his addled brain noticed how very attractive she looked, cheeks flushed, green eyes brilliant as the field on opening day.

41

"Why?" he managed.

"Why did I bring Tippy here? I'm sure that's what you're meaning to ask, right? It's the same thing I've been asking. I mean, why would someone bring a dog to a baseball arena?"

"Ballpark," Pete said.

"Right, ballpark. Anyway, why would someone, I mean why would I do that?"

Ag was staring at Gina as if she was a rare exotic animal.

"Tippy wouldn't eat, and I thought when you had your break time in between the baseball things, you could sit with her and, you know, encourage."

The baseball things?

Now Ag was smiling through his black beard. Cal had the sinking feeling the whole "Tippy at the arena" thing was going to make the rounds of the clubhouse at lightning speed. Ag was a crack catcher and a loose-lipped gossip.

Pete patted her arm. "It's okay, honey. It was an accident."

Ag offered a shy smile. "Yeah, this cowboy knows better than to take his eye off the ball. Totally his fault."

"No, I never should have brought Tippy. I should have tried tuna first. What dog can't resist tuna?"

"Or cheese puffs," Pete said. "She really went for those back on the boat."

Gina bit her lip. "Can I do anything for you, Mr. Crawford? Is there any way I can help?"

This girl, with her nutty dog ideas, could have just cost him his career. And what would Cal Crawford be if he wasn't a Major League pitcher? A dark thrill of fear crawled through him. He shut the thought down. "You've helped enough," he said, ignoring the look Pete blazed at him.

Her expression crumpled. There was no way to take the words back, so he looked away. His eyes narrowed on that overweight canine, pink tongue lolling and legs swimming enthusiastically as if she was ready for a vigorous game of fetch.

"I didn't realize what was happening," Gina said lamely. "Tippy got so excited when she saw it was you. She seems to have bonded with you already. Who knew she could cause so much trouble?"

He stared at the dog. She seemed to be smiling. "I did," he snapped as the cart carried him away.

Gina was more or less in control of her emotions the next morning when she arrived at Cal's house. He'd been admitted to the hospital and she had no idea what she should do aside from praying with all her might. *Lord, how could I have been so dumb?* This was a question she'd put to the Lord on a number of occasions, so she figured He was pretty used to it by now. *Please let Cal be okay.*

She fingered her cell phone again. Call him? Call her cousin? No, she'd decided that avoiding the inevitable conversation was the best policy, at least until she was officially fired. Let Lexi have a few more days of peaceful recovery. Right up to the moment Cal sent her packing, she was Tippy's caretaker and she would do her job.

"Hey, Tippy," she said, greeting the dog that was sprawled on the foyer floor in the patch of sunlight that streamed through the front window. "I brought you something."

Tippy offered a halfhearted wag, but did not resist as Gina slipped the pairs of socks on her paws, two pink socks in the front and two yellow on the back. "They've got the little gripper dots on the bottom so you won't slip, see?"

Tippy regarded her with those somber brown eyes. "Oh, honey," she said, sitting next to the dog. "I know you didn't mean to startle him. It was all my fault anyway. I'm supposed to be the one in charge. I never should have taken you to the arena or stadium or whatever it is."

"Ballpark," Cal said.

She jerked to her feet. He stood leaning on the doorway in jeans and a T-shirt. His face was a mess, bruised and battered, one eye swollen and a black shadow underneath. The wounds made her breath catch. Tippy roused herself to a sitting position, ears lifted.

Gina swallowed. "I didn't know you were home."

"Convinced 'em to let me go."

"Is there . . . um, will there be any lasting damage? I've been praying like crazy."

His gaze wandered. "Thanks, for the praying." Tippy hauled herself onto her paws and trotted over to Cal, tail wagging. He ignored the dog. "Why is it wearing socks?"

"She," Gina corrected automatically. "You said you were afraid she'd scratch the floor and she slips a lot."

"Why are they two different colors?"

"Because," Gina said, letting loose with a giggle, "socks come in twos, not fours. Or haven't you bought socks in a while?" She regretted her flippancy. When one is about to be fired, one should not be cracking jokes. She sighed. "Anyway, I got Tippy to eat a little something, but I had to mix in a cheese puff."

Cal just shook his head, wincing at the motion.

"I really am very sorry, Mr. Crawford. Really and truly."

"I know," he said, sitting on a chair and gesturing for her to do the same. "Please call me Cal. Mr. Crawford sounds like a high school math teacher or something."

She settled uneasily onto the sofa across from him as she prepared to be fired. On the coffee table was a crumpled section of the paper with a picture of Cal sprawled on the grass, dazed, a pudgy Tippy looking on. The headline said "Star Pitcher Toppled by Tippy." She winced. "If you want, I'm sure I can help you find a new dog sitter." *After I 'fess up to my cousin that I lost her a client.*

"Not necessary. Don't need a new one."

Hope sparked in her stomach. "Um, so, you mean I can still be Tippy's dog sitter?"

He hesitated, leaning forward, hands on his gangly legs. "No, I didn't mean that."

Uh oh.

"Gina, I appreciate what you've done for Tippy with the, uh, socks and everything, and I know you didn't mean any harm bringing her to the ballpark."

Gina could not hold back the smile. "You did it."

46

"Did what?"

"You called Tippy a *her.*" She sat back, triumphant. A huge step for both man and dog.

He blinked. "Right, let's just try and stick to the point here. Like I was saying, I appreciate all your help with Tippy, but it isn't going to work out."

So she was being fired after all. Muscles tightened up in her stomach. She forced a calm tone. "I understand. At least let me help you find someone else. I'm sure my cousin can recommend a replacement."

"That's not necessary."

"Did you find someone else to take her?" Tippy would be devastated without Cal. As it was, the hapless dog sat staring at him, mesmerized by his every move, but it would be better in the long run for her to live out her days with someone who loved her.

He sighed and ran a hand gingerly over his stubbled chin. "This isn't going well."

Gina stared at him. He picked an invisible piece of lint off his expensive jeans. Her stomach muscles tightened further. "Wait. If you don't need a new dog sitter and you're going to be busy with all that baseball stuff you were telling me about . . ." She clapped her hand to her mouth. "Oh no. Your career is over. Your occipital bone is mashed and you can't pitch anymore. I'm so, so sorry. Tippy and I are both sorry."

He shot her a bemused look. "No, no. My occipital bones are fine."

"Then how are you going to take care of Tippy? Are you giving her back to Pete?"

He looked down at his feet. "I'm taking her to the pound."

The words splatted there between them, like wet towels tossed on the locker room floor. "You can't do that," Gina said, with much more calm than she felt.

"It's the best way. I can't have her around here. Someone will come along and adopt her."

"No, they won't."

He eyed the dog. "She's not that bad looking. Nothing some weight loss wouldn't help."

"You're wrong," she said, voice quavering. "Tippy is thirteen years old and not in great shape. No one will take her. They will euthanize her." She said the word carefully, precisely, each terrible syllable spooling out between them.

"Gina . . ."

"Or she'll be shut in a wire cage on a cold cement floor. People will pass right by her on their way to the puppies. No one will adopt a geriatric dog." Her voice rose.

"Even if she's wearing cute socks."

"Let's keep this under control."

"I am under control. I'm just outraged. This is what I sound like when I'm outraged." The last bit came out loud.

He held up a palm. "You're getting hysterical."

"That's better than being an inhuman robot."

"I'm not an inhuman robot. It's called being practical."

"I'll take her."

"Your landlord won't allow it."

"I'll move."

"That'll take time."

"Tippy and I will live in my car until we find a spot," she squeaked.

He sighed. "You can't do that."

"Yes, I can. It's got a roomy backseat and cup holders." She realized tears were streaming down her face.

A look of horror broke across his face. "There's no need to cry. Please calm down."

"I can't," she cried. "This is wrong. Wrong, wrong, wrong."

He stood and held up his palms as if she was a wild animal he was keeping at bay. "Gina, I'm sorry it worked out this way, but try to think logically. It's for the best."

"It's because of your pride, isn't it?" She

49

flung a hand toward the newspaper. "A dog made you look silly in the paper and now you're going to have her destroyed."

"That's melodramatic."

"No, it isn't." She shot to her feet. "You're dumping her out like a piece of trash. How can you do that?"

"I'm taking her to the pound, not pitching her into the river."

Gina dashed a hand across her eyes. "Even if you don't care about Tippy, your mother loved her."

He flinched. "It's just a dog, an animal."

Gina felt like she'd been hit in the stomach. "Tippy's a *she* and *you're* a heartless egomaniac."

"I'm not," he said.

"Yes, you are, Cal Crawford, and I hope everyone in the arena knows it," she shrieked, slamming the door behind her as she fled.

FOUR

Cal fumed. Heartless egomaniac? What did the pet sitter know about his heart anyway? How could she know about something he didn't even understand? She'd been praying for him? He didn't want to hear it, since he wasn't speaking to God. No sense in anyone else doing so on his behalf. Trying to roll the tension from his shoulders, he shifted on the tile floor. Tippy sat complacently. The dog was probably too full to move after she'd hoovered up a bowl of kibble while he crouched next to her, hoping Luz would not arrive and see him there sprawled on the floor.

"Look, dog. You're going to be better off without me, I can promise you that."

Tippy snaked a pink tongue across her lips.

"All I care about is pitching. I don't want a dog. I told Pete and Gina right from the start." He realized he was engaging in

51

conversation with an animal. That crazy Gina was rubbing off on him. Best to have her out of the picture too. As soon as his doctor cleared him, he was going to have to put in double the effort to make sure he was up to speed. More resistance band stuff and maybe some weighted baseball work to boost his velocity training. The headline rolled through his head. *Toppled by Tippy.* His teammates had been Tweeting him jibes all day. Hilarious.

"But that's not the reason you've got to go," he found himself saying.

Tippy stared through cloudy eyes. "Mom . . ." he started. *Mom wouldn't want you to feel unloved,* he wanted to say, but he could not get past the first word. "This is ridiculous." He found Tippy's leash and clipped it on, and they made their leisurely way to the classic Mustang he'd restored. He opened the door and tipped the seat forward to usher her into the back.

She twitched an eyebrow and made no move to hop in. He grabbed her around the belly, but all her limbs had turned to rubber, refusing to be moved. After a few moments of wrestling which just made his head ache more, he flipped the seat forward again, intending to ease it further and make more room in the back for the flabby dog.

But before he'd had the chance, Tippy hurled herself into the passenger seat.

He gaped. "Seriously? You only want to ride in the front?"

Tippy settled down on the leather with a yip, ears flapping with excitement. "At least she's wearing socks," he grumbled, taking his place behind the wheel. Sliding sunglasses on to cover his bruised face, they made the drive to the pound and pulled up at the curb.

It didn't look like a bad place, all sleek lines and stone dog and cat statues poised outside. Clean and friendly. Tippy poked her head up and looked eagerly out the window, tail wagging as if she expected to see a park to play in. Something prickled in his gut.

"So, it's just gonna be for a while. Until someone adopts you. Some nice family with kids and stuff."

Her tail whipped back and forth, thumping against the car door.

But what if they didn't, like Gina predicted? His stomach knotted. Then she'd be well cared for at the shelter by people who knew what they were doing, he growled to himself. Experts, who actually liked dogs and chose to work with them. Tippy hopped out on her own when he opened the door, sniffing excitedly, nearly yanking the leash from his hand.

Tippy refused to be led up the steps, her nose firmly cemented to the smells she was snorking up. Stronger than she looked.

"Come on, Tippy," he hissed. It was getting later now, close to ten o'clock, and he didn't want to become a public spectacle. When Tippy steadfastly ignored him, he scooped her up and carried her to the top of the stairs. She waggled her short legs in the air, sending a yellow sock flying — which he was not about to stop and retrieve.

Faced with the door and a wildly squirming dog, he put Tippy down and yanked it open. The smell of antiseptic hit him, the hum of voices. He led her inside. Tail wagging, she yanked on the leash.

"You're gonna stay here for a while."

Another swish of the tail, eager gaze fastened on his face.

"I'll go check you in," he said, tying her leash to a chair. "Be right back." He walked a few feet away before he shot her another look.

Tippy was sitting now, her sad brown eyes fixed on him as if she had suddenly figured things out.

"It's not that you're a bad dog or anything."

Her head drooped, and now she would not look at him. He moved close again.

"I'm no good for you, Tippy." He got on one knee and stroked her soft ears, the graying head, the delicate bones underneath. "I've got to be one hundred percent about my pitching. You get that, right? You can understand how important that is? You don't get a second chance in this business. One shot, that's it. One."

Gina's words rang in his memory.

. . . your mother loved her.

Mom, his heart whispered, the ache rising inside. His mother was gone, and all her love and comfort and undying support was gone too.

"You're better off without me," he whispered into Tippy's ear as he left her there to take his place in line.

Gina paced the tiny bedroom that always smelled of onions. Mrs. Filipski, owner of the building and the pierogi store on the lower floor, had sent her to her room after she ruined two batches of dough which Mrs. Filipski described as "only fit for boot leather." Even the half dozen mashed potato pierogis that she'd insisted Gina take for lunch during her banishment did not do the trick. Gina was too grieved to eat one of the pillowy pockets.

How could Cal send his mother's elderly dog to the pound?

"And a man with oodles of money," Gina fumed. "He'd never even have to cross paths with the dog in that pretentious mansion of his."

Her phone buzzed. Lexi's name appeared on the tiny screen. She bit her lip, wondering how long she could put off telling her cousin that not only had she been let go, but her canine charge had been packed off to the pound. And by the way, she'd nearly crippled the Falcons' star pitcher. Fortunately, Lexi didn't enjoy social media, so with a bit of good fortune, she might not have seen the *Toppled by Tippy* headline. Yet.

Best to avoid the matter for a while.

Take a walk, Gina, she ordered herself. She reached for her jacket, annoyed to find she'd left it at the home of a certain flint-hearted pitcher. *Buy yourself another jacket.* But that one had been such a nice lemon color, with extra deep pockets and a liner that could be zipped in and out. It was a birthday gift from her mother who had visited and found the San Francisco temperatures inhuman compared with Florida, where the rest of the Palmer clan resided. It was one of her many attempts to persuade Gina to come home and take a job in her father's office, to be protected and taken care of like her parents had been trying to do since her first interminable hospital stay when she was only minutes old.

She imagined running into Cal again. Her face burned at the memory of what she'd hollered at him. *You've got nothing to be ashamed of.* Chin high, she sailed to the car, calling to Mrs. Filipski as she passed the shop. "I'm going to take back my jacket," she announced.

Mrs. Filipski looked up from her steaming pot of water, her glasses partially fogged. "From whom?"

"A horrible man."

"He treat you bad?"

"No. Not me." Cal, she had to admit, had done nothing to her personally. "He threw out an elderly, overweight female who never did anything but try to please him."

She waved a slotted spoon. "She's better off without him. You, too."

Gina sighed. Mrs. Filipski was not a fan of the male species since her own husband had left her at the Dulles airport fifteen years ago and flown back to Poland, where he'd promptly remarried. Gina had heard about it every day since she'd answered the help wanted ad six months earlier, desperate for a job after the bakery field trip debacle. Still, there were moments when she wondered if Mrs. Filipski might be softening a bit, especially toward Butch the mailman, who seemed to have an insatiable pierogi appetite.

Gina pulled her car from the weed-sprinkled lot behind the shop and drove to Cal's house. Ed let her in. He must have gotten wind of the disaster because both he and Bobby offered sympathetic smiles as they allowed her inside to retrieve her jacket. The quiet of the house tugged at her heart. There was no skittering of Tippy's feet on the floor, no excited snuffling or wheezing from the old dog. Gina blinked back tears. Hearing a familiar muttering in the kitchen, she decided to make her final goodbye.

Luz was at the cutting board, preparing a vegetable salad. The woman talked to herself, whacking apart a head of broccoli.

"Hello, Luz. What's the matter?"

Luz shook her head. "Hello, Gina. It's the Tweets."

"The what?"

She pointed the tip of the knife at her cell phone. "The Tweets. Mr. Cal is trending."

Gina was dumbfounded to discover that

Luz was tech savvy. "You Tweet?"

"Just to stay in touch with my sons, but I like to keep tabs on Mr. Cal. Just look what they're saying about him."

Gina squinted at the screen. The first Tweet was brutal. *#doghater #Falcons star pitcher #CalCrawford dumping #pet at the pound.* There was a picture of Cal bending over his Mustang, Tippy in his arms. Gina gasped in horror as she read some of the hundred-odd replies. They were not kind. Gina's throat closed up. As mad as she was at Cal, she would not wish this kind of vitriol on anyone. She peered again at the picture, throat thick.

Luz continued to rant. "Saying all those things about Cal. People who don't even know him."

What a disaster. Gina memorized the details in the photo. Tippy was cradled in Cal's arms with no inkling that the person she loved was about to discard her. It was the last time Gina would ever see the dog, she knew. Tippy's little socks, the droopy eyes. Gina's vision blurred again and she put the phone down, sucking in a breath to compose herself as her mind raced. Maybe she could find another place to rent that would let her take Tippy. But where could she find one for the pittance Mrs. Filipski charged on top of her pierogi duties?

She spotted the empty food bowl and water dish on the floor. With a leaden heart, she was bending to retrieve them when the door swung open and Tippy barreled into the kitchen.

"Tippy!" Gina cried, sinking to the floor and accepting the sloppy lick from the panting dog. Tippy stood expectantly, tail ricocheting back and forth. Gina rubbed the old dog's sides and shot a look at Luz. "How did she get here?"

Luz shrugged. "I don't know, but maybe we should do a Tweet to all those hateful people and tell them they're wrong about Mr. Cal."

Cal entered. "Don't bother. They've decided I'm a dog hater."

Gina shot to her feet. "What happened? I thought you took her to the pound."

He waved a hand and helped himself to a bottle of water from the fridge. Tippy ambled over and sat at Cal's feet, staring at him. Cal ignored the dog.

"Oh wait," she said, feeling her stomach sink again. "You saw the lady take your picture and you didn't want people to know what you were doing, so you brought her back."

Cal looked at her, brown eyes shining with

some emotion she could not decipher. "That's not what happened, but I know you and the rest of the world are never going to believe that."

"What did happen then?"

"Never mind. You got what you wanted. Tippy's here and you can take care of her if you want to. I'll be leaving next week anyway."

He turned away.

She was mystified. Something didn't fit. As much as he deserved to be lambasted by fans for abandoning Tippy, a notion crept into her mind. "Wait a minute." She took up Luz's phone and peered at the picture. Something warm bubbled up through her as the pieces clicked into place. A slow grin spread across her face.

"You changed your mind *before* that lady took the picture, didn't you?"

He stopped, one hand on the door. "Does it matter? Everyone thinks I'm a killer."

"Yes, it matters."

He rounded on her. "Why should it? I'm a pitcher. That's it. Who cares what kind of a person I am?"

"I do," she said quietly. "And so do you."

"You don't even know me," he said, voice low.

There was a stream of loneliness, of grief,

trickling under his words. She wanted to take his hand, to put her arms around him and let him rest his battered face against her shoulder. "I know you changed your mind about Tippy. You couldn't do it; you couldn't leave her there at the pound."

"How do you know that?"

Gina pointed to the cell phone screen. "The sock. Tippy's yellow sock. In the picture it's at the top of the stairs. You turned around and came back to the car and that's when the woman got your picture. You weren't taking her out of the car, you were putting her back in."

He rubbed a hand over his face. "I don't see what difference it makes why I did it."

She couldn't resist. She walked to him, raised herself up on tiptoe, and placed a gentle kiss on his unbruised cheek. The stubble on his chin tickled her lips, the warmth of his body lending some heat to hers. He tensed, but he did not retreat. Her palm rested on his cheek.

"It makes all the difference in the world," she said.

He sighed, so low and soft that she almost didn't hear it as he pulled out of reach. "Yeah. Well, anyway. Uh, could you still take care of the dog? I mean, if you've decided I'm not a heartless egomaniac?"

After she'd nearly killed him and had a full-on hissy fit in his living room, she could scarcely believe what she was hearing. "I would be thrilled to be Tippy's dog sitter." She rubbed Tippy's ears, sending the dog into a twitching pile of pleasure.

Luz offered a plate of immaculately arranged fruit. "You should eat, Mr. Cal. You haven't had a morsel in your stomach since last night. Look, there's a nice mango."

He stared at the plate. "Not hungry right now, Luz. Thanks, though. I'll eat it later, I promise."

"I'm going to take Tippy for a walk," Gina said. "Do you . . . would you like to come?"

Cal looked as though she'd suggested a trip to the gulag. "Got to call the lawyer about my mother's estate. You two have a nice time."

He left.

Luz looked forlornly at the fruit plate she'd labored over. "No breakfast. Again." She sighed. "What am I going to do with Mr. Cal?"

Gina stared in the direction Cal had taken. *Who cares what kind of man I am?* The words spoke of loneliness and loss.

She was overjoyed to be tending to Tippy, but who, she wondered, would take care of Cal?

FIVE

"I want to get on the mound." Cal shoved his hands in his pockets. The warehouse where he and the other pitchers did some offseason training was largely empty, except for some guys grunting through deadlifts and sprints on the treadmill. It was always a tricky balance for Cal in the offseason between the need to rest and rebuild his arm and the desire to throw every chance he got. This offseason was far worse for some reason. "I need some pitching time."

Pete took off his baseball cap, his scalp now covered by only the barest patch of stubble. When had he lost the puff of red hair that earned him all manner of teasing?

Cal met Pete for the first time when he started in the minors, a wet-behind-the-ears nineteen-year-old with a rifle of an arm and a heart shot to pieces. The old pitching coach had seen Cal at his finest, complete master of the 100-mile-an-hour fastball, and his most humble, repeatedly calling home his first season in the League, insisting to his mother that baseball was a mistake and declaring he was taking the next bus home. Pete became his father, his mentor, his nemesis, and his compass. Not true north, though. That spot was held by his mother. True north would always be Meg Crawford. His chest tightened.

"Are you listening to me?"

Cal blinked. "Yes. What?"

"I said you're not setting foot on that mound again until spring training and furthermore, you're not doing any aerobic work for another three, count them, thrreeeeeee days."

"I'm . . ."

Pete waved his hands as if he was swatting flies. "I know. Perfectly fine, hale and hearty, but guess what, Mr. Big Shot, you don't happen to have a medical degree, do you, last I checked?"

Cal huffed.

"Yeah, I didn't think so. With the amount we pay these team doctors, we might as well listen to them once in a while, shouldn't we? Skipper seems to think so anyway."

Coach Bruce — Skipper — would expect him to follow orders, but maybe Cal could convince him. "I'm feeling a hundred percent. I'll talk to Skipper."

"You've got something else to do." Pete sighed, the wrinkles around his eyes softening. "You've got time. Get it done, Cal."

Cal didn't have to ask what Pete meant. "Busy. I'll have someone else do it."

"No, you won't. You've got to go get the papers the lawyers need, box up the place if you're going to sell it. It's gonna hurt, but you can't move on with your life pretending she's not gone."

"I know she's gone," he snapped. "I'm not a child."

"Yeah, you're a man, but you got a mom-sized hole." Pete put a calloused fingertip on Cal's chest. "Right here."

Cal looked at the ground.

Pete cleared his throat. "I'm supposed to tell you that our people, you know, those mental health people, will talk to you, if you want."

"If it's not about pitching, I'm not talking."

"I know. Figured I'd say it anyways." He folded his arms. "Skipper wanted me to mention it."

Cal's head came up then. "Why? He's worried about my performance? I know the end of the season was bad, right before . . ." He shrugged. "Anyway, I'm getting it turned around. That's why I got to go back on the mound."

"Uh uh." The look Pete fired off was one Cal had seen many times before. The gray eyes were determined, immovable. Pete was putting his foot down. "You've got to do it, face it, take the pain and use it to get you where you want to go."

Cal knew about using pain, playing through it, in spite of it. That he could do. "It doesn't hurt, like when I was a kid with Dad." Cal scuffed a toe in the dirt. "Supposed to hurt, isn't it?"

Pete blew out a breath. "Not sure, but maybe it's like when the ball takes a hop and nails you when you're running. You keep running and feel the hurt later."

"Then I don't want to stop running," he mumbled.

Pete's hard face softened, the creases around his mouth gentling. "God's stopped your running for now, kid. He's calling the plays and He wants you to deal, so that's what you're gonna have to do. In a few weeks, we'll play some ball."

God had stopped his running? And taken his mom? Was there anything left to be stripped away? A cold numbness seeped through him. Pitching. It was all Cal had left, and he would die before he let God take that away too.

Pete clapped him on the back. "Take Gina and Tippy with you to the ranch."

Cal started. "Why would I do that?"

"Bunch of Tippy's dog stuff there. Gina will know what to do with it."

Take the dog and the pet sitter? For a moment, he felt the warmth of her palm on his cheek, her gaze that made something inside him go sideways. He shook it off, trudging out of the warehouse and driving back. Not wanting to face Luz and the agonizing prospect of a day with no baseball, he did not hurry. On the way the plan came together. He'd drive to Six Peaks, box up his mother's belongings, find the papers the lawyers were asking for, and be back by the day after next. The job needed to be done quickly and efficiently, without the confusing presence of Gina and Tippy.

Then it would be done and his mind would be fully on his game.

With a new spirit of purpose, he eased up the driveway to the house. As he passed the security gate, he noticed a van parked across the street. The guy behind the wheel was busy on his phone, cap pulled down over his eyes. He paid no attention as Cal went by.

Ed waved him through, chuckling.

"What's so funny, Ed?"

He jerked a thumb to the front lawn. "Most entertainment I've had in all my days working for you, sir. 'Cept of course the championship game year before last when you pitched a no-hitter."

Cal peered through the wrought-iron fence. He saw a flash of color, the blurry glimpse of a skirt. He parked quickly and made his way to the lawn.

Gina knelt on the grass, a tennis ball in her hands. Tippy lay down across from her. Both were staring so intently at each other that they did not notice Cal's approach.

"Okay, Tippy," Gina said, rubbing the ball as if she was polishing a diamond. "It's the bottom of the tenth, there's three outs already and it's all up to you. You've got to get the ball and run to home, remember? Ready?"

Tippy stood, tense with concentration.

"Fetch," Gina hollered tossing the ball onto the grass a few feet behind Tippy.

The dog leaped excitedly, circled twice, and sat down again in precisely the same spot.

Gina collapsed cross-legged onto the grass.

Cal could not hold back. He exploded into laughter. Gina leapt to her feet and Tippy

69

waddled over, tail wagging.

Gina folded her arms. "What is so amusing, Mr. Crawford?"

It took several more breaths before he was able to answer. "You know nothing about baseball."

"So? I'm not here to be your coach."

"And you're not making much progress coaching Tippy either." He wiped his eyes. "That was hilarious."

"It will take some time, that's all. She's a rookie at fetching." She brushed off her hands. "How was your day?"

The question surprised him. People asked about his performance, his training, but it had been a long while since anyone asked about his day. Something about it pleased him.

"Okay. Yours?"

"Pretty great. We went to the park and there was a man there who said Tippy had potential. As a matter of fact, the man said he went to college with you."

"Yeah?" The muscles in Cal's stomach tightened. "What's his name?"

She frowned, freckled nose squinching in thought. "Hmmm. I don't think he said."

He tried to keep his voice light.

"What'd he look like?"

"Tall, red hair . . ."

Now his stomach was good and truly clenched.

"You don't look happy. What's wrong?"

"Nothing. What did you say to him?"

"I just told him I worked for you. He has two dogs of his own."

Raised voices drew his attention. Ed was out of his guard station shack, striding to the front sidewalk fence where the van guy was now standing, camera pressed between the wrought iron bars.

"Get out of here before I call the cops," Ed shouted.

"Easy dude," the man said. "Cal and I are friends." He took off his cap and waved at Cal. "Hey, Cal. Talked to your girl this afternoon." He snapped another picture.

Cal took Gina by the arm. "Into the house."

Gina gaped. "That's the man I met in the park."

"Now, Gina," Cal commanded.

The guy got off one more picture before Ed reached him. Cal did not miss the guy's sly grin as he hustled Gina and Tippy into the house.

Gina sat on the sofa, mind whirling. "I don't understand what just happened."

Cal was pacing, muttering to himself as

he dialed his phone.

"Who are you calling?"

"The cops."

Gina stroked Tippy, who seemed to pick up on Cal's agitation. She whimpered, trying to jump up on the sofa. Her girth would not allow it, nor, Gina suspected, would Cal, so she slid down to the floor and tried to comfort the dog.

Cal finished his conversation and clicked off, running a hand through his short crop of hair.

"Who is that man?"

Cal shook his head. "His name is Tom Peterson and he's nuts. I have a restraining order against him. He must've been watching the house and saw you take Tippy to the park."

"How did he know about Tippy?" She groaned. "Oh right. Tippy's a Twitter sensation."

Thanks to my taking her to the arena, she thought.

"We played college ball together. He was a starting pitcher and he blew out his elbow. I took his spot, and he's decided somehow that I owe him something for that. He's unbalanced. Half the time he pretends he's my brother or something, and the other half he's ranting about me online. I've had to change my cell phone number twice because he gets hold of it somehow."

"Oh," she said, heart sinking. "He seemed so nice."

"He's not nice. He's crazy. Even went up to the ranch and harassed my mother." Cal paced in angry strides until he stopped to stare at her. "What did you tell him?"

She tried to recall. "Mostly we talked about Tippy, how she needs to wear socks in the house and such."

"Did he ask you details about your job?"

She flushed. "I thought it was just small talk."

"What?"

"He wanted to know my schedule, how many days and when I worked." Suddenly her own stupidity flooded over her. "He said he was hoping to get into the pet sitting business. I thought that was why he was interested."

Cal rubbed a hand over his eyes. "And you never suspected there was another reason?"

A lump in her throat rendered her unable to answer. She shook her head.

"You have to wise up," Cal snapped. "People are weird about fame. Like it or not — and believe me, I don't — I'm a celebrity. I have to be careful and if you're

73

going to work for me, you have to be careful too."

Her eyes filled and she looked at her lap. *Don't cry, you ninny.* Why must her emotions always flood to the surface at the least provocation? Tippy licked the tip of her nose. "I have trouble trusting the wrong people. I'd like to say that's because I got a rocky start and my parents sheltered me, but that's probably an excuse."

He frowned. "What kind of a rocky start?"

She waved a hand. "Never mind."

He let out a gust of air and his voice grew soft. He looked at the floor for a moment and let out a breath. "Please. I'd like to know. I understand rocky starts, believe me."

She shrugged. "I was born too soon, a micropreemie they call them, one pound and change."

"Man. That's less than four baseballs."

She managed a smile. "I never thought of it that way. I fit entirely in the palm of my father's hand, which really freaked him out. Actually it freaked both my parents out. My Nana held everyone together. She treated me like a regular baby, though a miniature-sized version. She took all the problems I had in stride and tried to see what I could do instead of what I couldn't." Gina sighed.

"I sure miss her."

She felt his eyes on her, heard the floor-boards creak as he shifted his weight. Why had she just shared her whole infant saga? He must think she was an idiot.

All of a sudden he joined her on the floor, long legs offering the perfect doggy plat-form. Tippy wasted no time in crawling aboard. Cal left her there, though he avoided her searching tongue.

"Your Nana sounds like a great lady."

"She was."

"Look, I'm sorry about how I spoke before," he said. "I didn't mean to come down on you so hard. You couldn't have known about Tom."

"But I should have wondered." Especially after her disastrous last relationship. The wrenching heartache came back, the man who let her love him and his son with her whole heart. The man who used and dumped her. "I'm too trusting. Always have been."

"It's not bad to trust people."

"Oh yes it is." The words blurted out. "Believe me. You can lose everything."

He took her hand. The gesture startled her, even as the strong fingers felt warm and comforting. "What happened?" he asked softly.

75

She looked into those liquid brown eyes and wanted to tell him everything. Of her humiliation, of the anguish she felt at being forever separated from a little boy she had come to adore. How she'd felt stupid and childish.

No, Gina. For once in your life be smart. Don't give all your feelings over to another man. Especially not a famous man from a completely different world. She detached her hand. He seemed embarrassed. "I'd rather not talk about it. I've shared enough for one day."

"Yeah, okay, sorry for prying."

"You don't need to be sorry," she said, forcing a strong tone. "I do. I won't let it happen again, blabbing too much to a stranger."

A gentle smile crossed his face. "Gina, have you ever met a stranger?"

She had to smile back. "I'm going to work on that."

He leaned back against the sofa and she did the same. It was the most relaxed she'd seen him since they'd met.

"Is that thing ugly?" he asked.

She raised an eyebrow. "What?"

He jerked a chin at the black glass sculpture on the sleek side table facing them. "That thing. I've never noticed it before, but it looks kinda ugly now that I'm at eye level."

She chuckled. "Do you want honest or polite?"

"Honest. I got enough people being polite all the time."

"My vote is ugly."

He laughed. "Mine too."

They sat for a few moments longer. She heard him take a deep breath.

"Would you come up to the ranch with me? You and Tippy?"

She stared.

"I think I'm gonna sell it, and I have to pack Mom's things, find some papers for the lawyers. There's plenty of bedrooms, cabin out back too." He got a faraway look in his eyes. "It's an incredible place."

A place where he felt at home, she read in the tenderness of his voice. Would it still feel that way to Cal with his mother gone?

"Why would you want me to come along?" She sighed, feeling a stab of shame. "Oh, wait. You think I'm going to get into trouble here alone, don't you?" She frowned. "I do bonehead things, but I can take care of myself and Tippy. Promise."

"It's not that. Pete figured maybe you could go through Tippy's stuff, and there's some of Mom's things . . ." His voice caught and he looked at her with eyes that shone with anguish. He cleared his throat. "Never mind. Bad idea. I'll check in with you when I get back." He eased Tippy off his lap and stood, looking out the window. "Cops are here. Guess I won't be leaving for a while."

He continued to stare as if he was seeing something else besides the perfectly tended lawns and the ornate wrought iron fencing.

"We'll go," she said suddenly.

He turned. "What?"

"Tippy and I will go. I just need to make sure Mrs. Filipski is okay with it. She's my landlady and she runs the pierogi store where I work."

He looked as though he wanted to say something. Then he abruptly closed his mouth and nodded. "Thank you. I'm glad."

She was not sure why, but she desperately wanted to see the ranch where Cal Crawford had left his heart. She nodded. "Tippy will be happy to spend some time with you."

And so will I, she thought with some astonishment.

SIX

Gina packed a bag for herself and Tippy and reported to the garage early the next morning. She was relieved to see no sign of Tom Peterson's van parked across the street, but there was a police car cruising the neighborhood.

Cal loaded her bag into the back of an enormous blue truck. It was cute, the way he did that, reaching for her duffel and relieving her of it before she asked. The gesture gave her a warm sensation in her stomach.

She took in the bulky old vehicle as he opened the door for her.

"Disappointed we're not taking the Porsche or the Mustang?" he said.

"Not really. My car has duct taped seats, so this is more up my alley."

He hoisted Tippy up into her lap. "This is a '66 Chevy C-10. Bought it on my own when I was seventeen. Rescued it from a junkyard, actually." His gaze wandered over the dinged chassis. Though the words were light, his shoulders were stiff, jaw tight. The drive to the ranch was something he would rather not undertake, even in his beloved truck.

They drove north for three hours before stopping for a fast-food lunch and a run around for Tippy. Cal made himself a finicky concoction at the salad bar and Gina ordered a large strawberry milkshake with whipped cream and a cherry.

"Don't you want the food part of the lunch?" he inquired. "Milkshakes are the dessert."

She shot him a look of disdain. "Dessert is the most important part and anyway, you're eating leaves for lunch so I don't think you're a credible advisor."

He chuckled and she somehow felt she had won a prize.

Cal kept his cap and sunglasses on and they ate at an outdoor table while Tippy sniffed every nook and cranny. Gina relished her milkshake, draining it to the dregs. Cal picked at his salad.

"Luz would say you should eat," Gina said.

He nodded and applied himself mechanically to the greens without any apparent enjoyment until a lady with curly hair and full cheeks approached.

She sidled up, clutching a piece of paper in one hand and her young son's shoulder in the other. "Excuse me," she said. "Are you . . . ?"

Cal looked up.

"You are." She squeezed her son's hand. "It's Cal Crawford," she said. "I knew it. I wasn't sure at first, but then I saw the dog. That's Tippy, right?"

Cal gave her a polite smile. "Yes, ma'am."

"Could I possibly get your autograph? My son is starting Little League and his dad will just flip when I tell him we saw you."

Cal took the piece of paper and got down on one knee next to the child. He scrawled his autograph on the paper. "What's your name?"

"Max," the child said, barely above a whisper.

"And I'm Leslie," his mom chimed in. "Could you possibly write 'Best of luck to the Cardinals this season'?' " she asked. "That's Maxie's team."

Cal smiled. "Sure," he said as he scribbled.

"This is so thrilling," she gushed. "I can't believe we're actually here talking to Cal Crawford. You're taller than you look on TV."

Cal chatted with the boy and Gina saw immediately how he put the child at ease. "So what position do you play, Max?"

"First base," the boy replied. "My dad taught me." He watched Cal with wide eyes. "Did your dad teach you?"

Gina saw Cal's mouth twitch, a flash of pain that surfaced and disappeared. "No, Max. My mom is . . . my mom got me started, and my Uncle Oscar."

"And this is Tippy? I didn't believe those Tweets in the first place. I knew you weren't the type to get rid of a sweet old dog," Leslie gushed, reaching down to rub Tippy's ears. Tippy basked in the attention. Leslie shot Gina a sly look. "And you're Mr. Crawford's special someone?"

Gina's face went hot. "Oh, no. I'm Tippy's special someone. I'm the dog sitter."

The woman gave Tippy a final pat. "How nice," she said, in a tone that indicated she didn't believe a word of it.

Cal finally disentangled himself from Leslie and Max. "We've got to go now, but it's been a pleasure, ma'am."

She tried to keep up as he hustled to the car, Tippy trotting along behind. They were not quick enough. A half dozen patrons of the restaurant approached, clamoring for autographs.

With a sigh, Cal plastered on a smile, the car keys still dangling from his fingers. "Time for a meet and greet," he said.

Gina saw no more than a blur as Tippy launched herself higher than Gina would have ever thought possible, leaped into the air, and snatched the keys from Cal's hand.

"What'd she do that for?" Cal said, stunned. Tippy tore off into the empty field behind the restaurant.

Cal pursued, long legs quickly outpacing Gina as a merry chase began. The kids in the group joined in as Tippy zigged left and zagged right. All around them the bystanders recorded the whole adventure with their iPhones.

"Tippy," Gina called when she got a breath. "Stop."

She remembered from her cousin Lexi that you had to stick with a dog's known vocabulary. They'd not covered *stop* to date. A boy ahead of her turned quickly and Gina almost tumbled over him.

"Tippy, sit!" she hollered as loud as she could.

Ignoring her completely, the dog leaped and whirled, wiry body contorting in incredible fashion.

"Sit!" Cal boomed.

Tippy sat, her wedge of a bottom dropping immediately onto the scraggly grass.

The crowd of dog wranglers staggered to a stop, the children sitting next to Tippy to get a turn petting the panting dog.

Cal snatched up the slobbery keys from where Tippy had deposited them, staring. He reached down and gathered Tippy up. "Now I see what Pete meant about the car key thing. That was pretty good speed for a dog with four-inch legs."

"Gonna take her to the pound again?" a voice called out.

A heavyset man in an Oakland A's jacket stood watching, arms folded. "Don't know why you all are goggling over Crawford here. Guy's been slumping big-time, and plus he's a dog hater."

Cal shook his head. "There's always one in every crowd," he muttered.

Leslie strode up to the man. "He is not a dog hater. That was a misunderstanding, as you can see. Tippy goes everywhere with Cal, and every athlete slumps, for your information."

"They got pictures of him taking that dog to the pound," the man insisted. "I saw it."

"Cal Crawford is a good man," Leslie said.

"He sure ain't a good pitcher," the man said, turning away.

"He's a two-time Cy Young award winner,

84

you dolt!" Leslie called after him.

There was no expression on Cal's face as he waved to the group and headed back to the truck. Once again he opened the door for Gina and handed over the exhausted dog.

Gina cuddled Tippy, who looked very satisfied with her performance. "You're naughty, Tippy. Don't look so proud of yourself."

If dogs could smile, Gina would have sworn that was what Tippy did before she settled her head on Gina's knees and fell asleep.

Cal drove out of the parking lot in silence, face shuttered.

"Does it make you mad?" she asked.

"What?"

"When they say you're not a good pitcher?"

"No. That comes with the job. You're always going to get hecklers."

He'd left something unsaid. "What's bothering you then?"

"Nothing."

"Not nothing."

He shot her a look, brown eyes intense. For a moment, she thought he was going to ignore the question. "The woman. Leslie."

"She was nice. A huge fan of yours."

"Yeah."

Again the hesitation.

"She said you were a good man."

His brow furrowed. "That's what I mean. She doesn't know that."

Gina wasn't sure what to say.

"She doesn't know what kind of a man I am. No one does."

"They feel like they do because you're famous."

He talked as if he hadn't heard her. "They know how I pitch and field and how much money I make and how many times I was traded and my ERA and every single stat of my whole life in the majors, but . . ." He trailed off.

Tippy snuggled deeper into Gina's lap. "They don't know the real Cal Crawford?"

"No one knows me." He pressed his lips together. "I don't even think I know me anymore."

"God knows you," she blurted out. "And He loves you." Ack. Had she really said that out loud? He already thought she was a nut, and now add religious nut to the list. "I mean," she hastened on, "He made you. Nothing about you is a surprise to Him. My Nana said so, and she knew God better than anyone else I ever met."

He shifted, making the seat creak. Tippy

opened one eye and closed it again. "That's what my mom would have said too."

"But you don't believe it?"

"She always told me God made me great."

"You are great, Cal," Gina said, touching his shoulder. "You've done amazing things in your life."

"But what if I don't anymore? What if I fail? Guy back there's right. My pitching isn't so hot lately. So if God's gonna take that away, what do I have left?"

Gina stroked Tippy's boney head. *For once, think before you blurt.* What would her Nana have said? The woman who made the initial introductions between Gina and God during those long hours in the NICU with Gina's mom sick and her father too overwhelmed to do much more than pace? She chewed her lip and shot a glance at Cal. None of this had been in the dogsitter manual Lexi had typed up for her under "relating to the pet owner."

"Well," she started cautiously. "Maybe when your mom said God made you great, she wasn't talking about your pitching."

He started a bit, as though he'd just caught another ball to the face, eyes dancing between her and the front windshield. Then he turned his full attention to the road. "No. Pitching is what I was made to do. I am a great pitcher and God's not gonna take that away from me. I won't let Him." His tone was hard, mouth pinched into a tight line which made him look much older than his twenty-eight years.

Gina thought about the things she had lost and her heart squeezed tight. Matthew's soft hair and how it tickled her chin. The way he would run to her when she met him at the park, his face lighting up. Playdough time. Kissed boo-boos. Bedtime storybooks.

But she wasn't his mother and never would be. Now his hair tickled Vivian's chin and the stick figure drawings adorned her refrigerator. Gina should be glad. God wanted mothers to be reunited with their sons. But where had that left Gina? Lost. Hurt, but not forgotten. Not by Him. It was the only truth she knew for certain. As much as she'd wanted it, God hadn't meant Gina to be a mother to Matthew. It hurt. Still. But she'd been changed and blessed while it had lasted. Cal was still hurting too much to hear that truth, she figured.

Cal shot a glance at her. "Um, sorry. That got heavy."

Yeah. Heavy.

In spite of the weird day they'd had so far, Cal's spirits lifted as they drove up the steep road to Six Peaks Ranch in Humboldt County. Cal wasn't an imaginative guy. In school when faced with writing a creative story, he'd labored on for pages describing every detail of a nine inning baseball game until the teacher took his pencil away, but now he could smell the sundried alfalfa, though the bales were long since sold and the land gone fallow. He heard the blatting of the goats, jostling one another as they headed for milking, and most of all, he could taste the succulent ripe peaches that had hung heavy from the tree in seasons past. A craving for peaches nearly over-whelmed him in that moment.

Trees crowded the road, and the wheels jostled over the gravel which Cal automati-cally noted had worn thin in spots. Good thing the winter had been dry or the truck might be hubcap deep in mud. The drive paralleled a split rail fence. He stomped on the brake so hard, Gina slid forward on the seat.

"Sorry."

And then he was out of the car, forgetting to open the door for her, approaching the old mare cropping grass, tawny head hung over the fence.

"Hold on a minute, Tip," he heard Gina say as she opened the door. Tippy lost no time in joining him.

"My old girl," Cal said, stroking the horse's muzzle. The animal blew out a soft breath as Cal leaned his forehead against hers.

Tippy danced up, sproinging into the air as if on springs, until the horse leaned down and allowed her a welcome lick. She blew a breath onto the dog that sent her ears fluttering.

Gina stood, eyes wide. "I guess you all know each other."

"This is Potato Chip. We grew up together."

Gina stroked the silky shoulders as the horse nosed around. "Potato Chip?"

"My mother's idea. They were both nutty for junk food. Chip here always knew when Mom had a baggie full in her pocket."

"And no amount of scolding ever did change your stubborn mother's mind about proper horse food."

They both jerked around. Cal allowed himself a breathless moment to take in the older man, still tall and erect, discounting a slight stooping of the shoulders. He sported a full head of silver hair, legs strong and straight in their faded jeans, a sweat-stained Falcons baseball cap in his hand.

Something tight released inside Cal and

suddenly he felt as if he could take his first full breath in months, like a drowning man sucking in that first lungful after being rescued. He clasped the man in a tight hug. The hard thumps on Cal's back spoke more love than any words they might have mustered between them.

"Staying out of trouble, Cal?"

"Yes, sir." He gave a final squeeze before releasing the hug. "Gina, this is my Uncle Oscar."

"So nice to meet you." Gina extended a hand.

Cal guided her palm into Oscar's. He took in her surprise. "Uncle Oscar is blind."

"Almost blind," he said, folding her hand between his two calloused palms. "I can still see shadows and I'm pretty sure you're a lovely young shadow, aren't you?"

Gina laughed in that silvery, bubbly way that made Cal want to join in.

"I'm a little travel worn, but I appreciate the compliment."

"And here's your mother's nutty dog," Oscar said, leaning over to offer his fingers for a Tippy greeting. The dog whined in pleasure, nearly falling over with wild enthusiasm. "Weirdest dog ever to pee in a pasture, but Meg loved her."

Cal swallowed a sudden thickening in his

throat. "Should have left Tippy here at the ranch."

"Nah," Oscar said. "Tippy don't stay put. Hard to keep tabs on her after Sweets got sick. Grateful when Pete took her after the funeral."

Cal's heart folded in on itself again. "I'm sorry I haven't called in a while. How is Sweets?"

"Good. You stayin' a while?"

"Couple of days."

"Tell you what. How about I bring her on up to the big house tonight and we have ourselves a little dinner together? Sweets would like nothing better. We can jaw a bit and bore the socks off this lovely lady."

"Yes, sir," Cal said. "I'll fix us something."

"No thanks, Cal. I've tasted your cooking before. Sweets will whip us up a meal."

"But she's . . ."

He stopped Cal with a palm. "You don't know anything about it, son. Sweets and me been married going on sixty-two years now, and I can read that woman like a book. She'd have my ears if I edged her out of cooking a meal for you."

"I'd be happy to help," Gina said.

"It's settled then." A crafty look came over Uncle Oscar's face. "Handy your coming here just at this time. I got a favor to ask of

92

you, Cal."

Cal raised an eyebrow. "Am I going to like it?"

"Don't matter 'cause you're gonna do it anyway."

Cal laughed again. True. He would never refuse a favor to Uncle Oscar. He would never refuse him anything.

"Gotta go. Fred's giving me a lift into town." Oscar tipped his battered hat to Gina and strode away, his fingers trailing along the split rail fence.

Gina inhaled a deep breath that lifted her slender shoulders, sunlight gilding her blonde hair. "Your Uncle Oscar is perfect," she said. "Just the sort of man I'd imagine in this place. You two are really close, aren't you?"

"He raised me since I was a kid."

"What happened to your father?" She clapped a hand over her mouth. "Uh oh. Filter didn't engage. I'm hearing my mother's voice inside my head telling me that was nosey and inappropriate."

He could not help but smile at her look of chagrin. "Probably was. Anyway, when I was eight, I lost my dad."

"Oh, I'm so sorry. Did he . . . pass away?"

Cal flicked back to the nights he sat awake at his window, curtain pulled pack, waiting

93

for that green Buick to reappear, knowing his mother was doing the same thing. "Might as well have," Cal said.

He saw her recoil at the bitterness in his voice, but he could not hold back the rest. It spilled over from the well of anger that never ran dry.

"My dad left us, and he never looked back."

SEVEN

Gina was surprised at the size of the ranch. Forty acres, she'd managed to pry from Cal as he showed her to the main house, a single level with wood siding and a massive spray of vine trying its best to devour the whole structure.

"Got two bedrooms and there's a guest house."

"Was it a working ranch?"

He raised his chin, offended. "Sure it was. We grew alfalfa hay, raised livestock and chickens. Believe it or not, I even learned how to make goat's milk cheese."

She tried to picture the Falcons' multi-million-dollar star pitcher milking goats. "You don't read that in *Sports Illustrated.*"

He grinned. "Yeah, but it was good training. Wrangling a ball's a lot easier than milking an angry goat."

They passed a fat calico cat sitting on the sun-bleached porch. Tippy trotted over and wagged her tail. The cat swiped out a paw and whacked Tippy on the snout. Tail tucked, Tippy ran behind Gina with a whine.

"Mean cat," Gina said.

"That's why his name is Crabs. Tippy's been trying to make friends with that cat for months. Don't know when she's going to learn that Crabs just doesn't like her and never will."

"Oh, Tippy will wear her down someday." She wagged her finger at the cat. "Crabs, you will succumb to Tippy's natural charm sooner or later. Resistance is futile, cat."

Cal stopped, fingers on the door handle. "You really believe that, don't you?"

"Yes. Tippy's charm is limitless."

He raised a skeptical eyebrow at the cowering dog. "Do you always see the sunny side of things?"

"Whenever I can."

"Where'd you get that outlook?"

"Probably I was just born that way. Maybe I spent so many hours in the NICU with Nana she rubbed off on me."

"Are your parents like that?"

"No. My dad's very serious — he's a urologist. So's my older brother. They run a practice together. Mom's a medical re-searcher. Very left-brained and all that. I'm the oddball of the family."

"Didn't want to go into medicine?"

She sighed. "My parents desperately wanted me to. I tried, I really did, but I just wasn't that interested in math and science. I have memory problems and no amount of tutoring could change that, much to their dismay."

"How'd they handle that?"

Her cheeks warmed. "They tried to arrange internships for me, jobs in the various family businesses, passed me around from relative to relative. At this point, I think they are resigned to my failures. My mother tells people I'm 'taking time to consider my options.' She's still hoping I'll miraculously morph into a doctor or lawyer or something. They thought the teaching idea was crazy anyway."

"Why? You're great with people. Why not teach?"

"Something to do with little pay, long hours, and the fact I was born into a family of doctors, so how could I not inherit the medical mantle?"

"I've met a lot of doctors," Cal said. "You're too compassionate to be a doctor, and I mean that in a good way."

He thought she was compassionate? Something swirled inside her stomach that made her cheeks burn even more. "Compassion isn't as highly regarded as a medical degree in my family."

"It should be." His eyes lingered a moment on hers before she looked down and fussed over Tippy, who was trying to both get into the house and stay out of feline range.

"Just a minute, dog," Cal said, holding the animal back with one foot while he opened the door. Tippy scrambled inside and would have tripped Gina if Cal hadn't grabbed her arm to steady her.

"Tippy's a menace," he said, but his voice was soft.

They passed into a front hallway with an old hat stand on which hung a woman's nubby knit sweater in a vivacious pink. The striped wallpaper had probably been cheerful when it was hung many years before, but now it was faded and peeling along one seam. In the kitchen, winter sunshine shone in through the open curtains onto old appliances and a gouged wooden table with a few magic marker lines marring the surface.

Gina could picture a little boy Cal sitting there, drawing, dreaming of playing baseball in the big leagues. How many young boys fantasized about the same thing, and how precious few achieved their dreams? Yet for all his amazing achievements, Cal was far from a happy man. She wondered if being at the ranch would help him come to grips with his unhappiness, or make it worse.

At the moment, a look of longing was creeping over Cal. He pointed out the window toward a tree-clustered swell of land. "Over there's Slip Rock Creek. It's the best thing about this ranch. Never runs dry, even in the summer."

"Your own creek. That's something."

"Yeah. I used to fish there every chance I got until my mom begged me to stop for a while and give the fish a chance to recover."

"Poor fish."

"I've got some ferocious fishing skills." He laughed, eyes sparkling as they swiveled to her. "Maybe . . . uh, I could show you the creek, if you want."

"That would be great," she said.

He nodded. "So in the back is the garden, but I don't think anyone's tending it. My uncle does what he can to keep up the place, but it's too much for him. Uncle Oscar and Sweets live in a trailer on a piece of property about two miles up the road." He showed the way past a small sitting room, done in worn tan carpet with comfortable, overstuffed furniture. No TV, the walls crowded with photos which Gina intended to get a good look at later.

"Down here are the bedrooms. I thought, maybe, if you want, you could stay in my old room."

They stopped at a small room plastered with baseball pennants, home to one full bed and an old wooden dresser. She peered at a shelf filled with trophies and picked one up. "Hey, you've even got one here for Boy Scouts."

"Won the Pinewood Derby. Mom helped me build the car. Called it the Thunder Racer." He shook his head. "I don't know why I remember that."

Again, the pain shimmered in his eyes.

She replaced the trophy very carefully back on the shelf, thinking with sadness that Matthew would probably do the same thing, build a car and race it. Win or lose, she would never know how it turned out. Matthew was back with his mother, where he belonged. She should be happy for him and she was. Mostly.

Cal shrugged. "Sorry about the decor. I never got around to making it a grown-up room. I stayed here until I went off to college." His gaze drifted around the space. "Small, but it's got its own bathroom."

"This will be fine," she said. "I can memorize the teams, study up on my baseball knowledge."

Another faint smile. "And man could you use it."

She elbowed him in the ribs as she passed.

Tippy dashed ahead of them, nails scrabbling on the scarred wood floor. *Good thing I packed her socks,* Gina thought.

Tippy sprinted to the end of the hallway, where she whacked her snout against a closed door. Ricocheting off with a dull thud, she sat down, stunned. Gina went to comfort her. "Maybe you should learn to knock first, honey."

"She's not used to the door being shut. Never was when my . . ." Cal paused. "I mean it always used to be open." After a moment of hesitation, Cal opened the door.

A waft of stale air hit them, laced with the faint scent of fragrance. A woman's perfume? Hairspray? Tippy did a quick trot around the perimeter of the room, nose to the floor. She investigated the bathroom and closet before she skittered to the bed, plowing up the foam steps that must have been purchased for her. Nose quivering, she sniffed every square inch of the mattress. Puzzled, she paused and did another full circular scan of the bed.

Gina realized what was going on. Her mouth went dry as Tippy continued her fruitless search.

Looking from Cal to Gina, her confusion seemed to make her jowls sag even more than usual. After a long moment, she circled three times and sank down. Fixing filmy brown eyes on the humans, she let out one soft whine. The sound was filled with yearning and loss. It spoke of a void that would not be filled this side of heaven, a broken heart that would never heal. Tippy laid her head down on her paws.

Gina's throat thickened and her eyes began to fill. *Don't cry, Gina. Don't make it worse for Cal.* She forced in a steadying breath. When she decided she was as in control as she was going to get, she risked a look at Cal to gauge his reaction.

He had already gone from the room.

"Tippy," Gina coaxed. She sat on the bed, patting the mattress next to her, but Tippy remained still, dead center.

"Come here, baby."

Still Tippy would not come.

Gina finally crawled over to meet her, nestled near the limp creature.

"Your mama is gone. I'm so sorry," she whispered against the top of Tippy's head, scooping her up and rocking the dog like an infant. Could Tippy still catch Meg's scent? Was the old dog listening hopefully for her footsteps in the hallway?

The thought made her tears spill over. She tried to cry quietly, so Cal wouldn't hear in case he was close by.

You just can't explain death to a dog, she thought. And why should a dog understand things that people sometimes couldn't?

The closet doors were open and empty of clothes. The old chest with drawers slightly ajar was too. At least Cal had been spared the need to pack her clothes.

Or was it good to be spared that? She wondered if Cal would be able to start healing when he was trying so hard to stay away from the truth.

"Lord," she whispered, caressing the dispirited dog, "mend Cal's broken heart." She pressed another kiss on the dog's boney head. "And take care of Tippy's heart, too."

Tippy put her cold nose against Gina's chin as she carried her out of the room and closed the door behind them.

Gina didn't actually unpack anything, since they were only due to stay a few days and it felt odd to be opening drawers and closets in Cal's boyhood room. She rested for a while, until the buzz of a text message woke her from a doze.

Her heart squeezed when she saw that it

was from Bill.

Checking on you. How are things?

She wondered what had spurred him to message her. Dark hair, spiffy dresser, Ivy League all the way, keen sense of humor, she'd loved Bill from the moment they'd met at the ice cream social at Mount Olive Christian School where she'd been subbing. Yes, she'd loved Bill, but it was his five-year-old son, Matthew, who had left such a big empty spot in her heart that she feared it would never heal.

How should she answer a man who had reunited with his classy, corporate CEO ex-wife and dumped her over a cup of coffee while his son colored with his crayons and watched? She wasn't sure how Vivian, the former ex, would feel about Bill texting her. She deleted the message and was about to turn off her phone when it buzzed again.

Matthew started Little League. A photo popped up of Matthew in his white baseball uniform, pristinely clean, freckled face grinning. She peered close to catch every tiny detail, surprised to feel her eyes filling again. He'd probably sent the picture as a kindness, but it stung to see the boy she loved and could not touch.

A soft knock at the door startled her. Blinking hard, she stowed the phone in her pocket and opened the door.

Cal stood there, looking uncertain. "Are you . . . okay?"

"Yes," she said with a vehement shake of the head. "Sure. What's up?"

"I was, you know, looking through some things in the study, and I figured maybe you'd want this. For Tippy."

He thrust a cardboard box into her hands. She peered inside. There were a few dog training books, a long and short leash, and a box of liver-flavored dog treats.

"That's great. I'm sure the training books will help. Can I give you a hand in the study?"

He shrugged. "Nah. I can do it. Just going to box everything up and leave it until we need to show the place."

"Have you put in on the market?"

He looked pained. "Been meaning to make a call."

"Cal?"

"Yeah?"

"Can I ask why you don't keep the ranch? You obviously have so much fondness for this place."

"Keep it?" He blinked. "Don't have time to run it, and Uncle Oscar isn't up to it anymore."

"Not to sound snide, but you have the

money to hire someone else to do it."

"Time to move on. Got to focus on baseball and not worry about this old place that's falling to pieces. This isn't home anymore." His brown eyes drifted to the shelves behind her, the old tattered quilt.

"It doesn't seem like San Francisco is your home either," she said as gently as she could.

His eyes skimmed over the faded pennants and the kid trophies. "Home is anywhere there's a pitcher's mound."

Anywhere. And nowhere.

There was a knock on the front door.

"Where's my rascal of a nephew?" a soprano voice sang out.

Cal grinned. "Ready to meet Sweets?"

"I wouldn't miss it."

EIGHT

Cal bent down to kiss his aunt's forehead, careful not to muss the poof of dark hair held in place with a complicated network of bobby pins. She was impeccably dressed, as always, in neat slacks and a purple sweater set, a strand of pearls around her neck. The sight of the pearls made him swallow hard. His mother had worn a matching strand until the day she died, the twin sisters having been given them on their sixteenth birthday by the father who adored them. Papa, they'd called him, the man who'd built Six Peaks Ranch.

"Look at you," Sweets said, peering up at him. Her head was just about level with his shoulders. She plucked at the front of his T-shirt. "Skin and bones. Doesn't your team give you food money?" She peered closer. "And what happened to your face? You're all black and blue."

"Took my eye off the ball." He shot a look

at Tippy, who stared vaguely. Gina blushed that cotton candy pink that fascinated him.

"Good thing you aren't a professional bowler," Oscar put in.

He laughed. "Yes, sir. Sweets, this is Gina. She's taking care of Tippy for me."

Sweets eyed Gina and smiled before her gaze swiveled to the dog. "Oh, put that horrible animal on the floor, honey. Who knows where those dirty paws have been?"

Gina reluctantly set Tippy on the ground. Tippy immediately rolled over, presenting her tummy for Sweets to scratch, stubby legs churning the air.

"Oh phooey, dog. You'll get no fawning over from me. You know where you belong." Sweets stretched out a perfectly manicured finger. "Right now."

Tippy shot Sweets a look which communicated wounded pride, even to Cal, and then waddled over to a plump cushion in the kitchen corner and flopped there.

"My sister would treat that critter like the Queen of Siam," Sweets said, "but not this lady. Dogs are meant to herd sheep and cattle, not take up space in the house. Besides, I wasn't crazy about her former owner either. Never took the time to teach Tippy that she is an animal, not a person." She extended a hand to Gina. "Very pleased to meet you, Gina. I hope Cal hasn't been too grumpy with you. He takes himself way too seriously now that he plays a game for a living."

Cal laughed. "How have you been feeling, Sweets?"

She took an apron from the peg on the wall. "Right as rain. I did a grapefruit cleanse which perked me up after that nasty flu. It's all about eating healthy, you know. Oscar and I have been getting bushels of greens and fresh fish."

He caught Uncle Oscar's expression. Oscar, he knew, understood the gravity of Sweet's situation. Three times she'd battled breast cancer. The last time, her survival was not certain and the doctors said it was likely a matter of time before the cancer would win, as it had in her sister.

Sweets was constantly switching up their diet according to the latest research on healthy eating. Oscar pretended not to know about the candy wrappers that she hid under her upholstered recliner. He made sure there was always candy in the cupboard, and he never pointed out the hypocrisy. It was one of the many idiosyncrasies that kept them married. If Cal ever had a shot at matrimony, he'd remember. Not that he would ever marry, he figured. He didn't have the genes for a marriage like Sweets and Oscar.

"Oscar's stomach was rumbling all the way over here," Sweets said. "I'll just get started on some dinner, shall I? Then you can tell us all about everything and we can get to know your pretty friend here."

More blushing from Gina.

"That would be great," Cal said. "How can I help?"

"Just keep that dog out of the way," she said.

Cal grimaced. "Sorry, but that dog doesn't listen to me most of the time."

Sweets laughed. "Typical female."

"You sure you don't need me to get down some ingredients from the cupboard for you?" he teased.

Sweets huffed, extracting a long metal grabber from the lower cabinet, poking him in the chest with it. "I can do for myself, Cal Crawford. I'm sure this young lady will help me, won't you, Gina?"

"I will, but the only thing I know how to make is pierogis."

Sweets cocked her head. "That begins with a P so I can't cook that."

Gina looked confused.

Cal chuckled. "Sweets didn't know how to cook when she and Oscar got married, so she bought a cookbook and practiced every recipe in alphabetical order of the index. Mastered every recipe until the end of the M section."

"I figured that was enough," Sweets said.

"It is," Oscar added.

"It's enough for me too," Cal put in. "I could live on your meatloaf for the rest of my life."

"Exactly what I'm making for dinner because I know that's your favorite."

"Better than pitching a no-hitter."

She smiled and he bent to give her a hug. His hands felt enormous on her fragile shoulders. Had she always felt so small and delicate? As if one careless movement might break her? She and Gina started to work and he stepped away, standing next to Tippy and Oscar. For a moment, he watched the project unfold. Sweets wrapped Gina in an apron with roosters printed on it, the strings circling twice around her small waist. The two chatted as if they had been friends for a long time.

It was good, he realized, to see two women bustling around the worn kitchen, to hear the squeak of the refrigerator door mingled with the high-pitched voices. His mother would have enjoyed that blessing, chatting and laughing with them.

Blessings? He hadn't thought about them in a long time. He let the silvery tones wash over him for a minute more and then he headed to the study, his uncle following.

Files were stacked in precarious piles on the tiny secondhand desk. A narrow bookcase was jammed with everything from cookbooks to bulging photo albums. It was a dusty mess, according to Cal's ultra-neat standards, but the room had a window looking out on the garden which had been his mother's joy. What were those tall frilly flowers she'd loved? Hollyhocks, like bits of crepe paper that unfurled in fantastic fashion on thick stalks. Were there any still growing? He could not tell because of the overgrown shrubbery.

I'll cut it back before I leave.

A dog cushion, neatly dented in the middle from Tippy's bulk, was positioned on the hardwood to catch the sunlight. Next to the window was a Falcons season calendar. His stats were noted in tiny block letters next to each game.

He read one of the squares. Four strikeouts over eight scoreless innings. Gave up only three hits and a walk. He'd been on fire that game. His mother would have been proud. So proud. Last few games of the season was another story. The last calendar box was empty. No stats. He'd wanted to be with her that day, but she'd insisted he pitch.

"I'll watch it on TV, Cal," she'd said on the phone. "You have fun, sweet boy."

Sweet boy. His eyes pricked and he blinked them hard. Not sweet anymore, nor a boy.

Oscar shoved his hands in his pockets.

"Dusty in here," Cal said. He picked up a file. Tax returns from ten years prior. "I guess Mom was trying to put things in order."

Oscar shifted, leaning against the doorframe. "She . . ." he cleared his throat. "She had some help the last six months."

Cal smiled. "You and Sweets?"

He snorted. "I'm not the guy for paperwork. Meg didn't want to ask Sweets to help either, her still recovering from the chemo and all."

Something in his tone drew Cal's full attention. "Who then?"

Oscar rubbed a hand over his shaven chin. "Been meaning to talk to you about it, but you haven't been around. Not the sort of thing you mention in a phone call."

Cal put down the file and moved closer to his uncle. "Who was helping my mom, Uncle Oscar?"

A long moment passed. "Cal . . ."

"Tell me," he said through the sense of dread that trickled through his insides.

"Your father," Oscar said. "Mitch."

Gina was good and truly amazed when the meatloaf came out of the oven, warm and succulent. Tippy yipped her appreciation, swiping a long pink tongue over her lips.

"You shush," Sweets said. "This is food for people."

Tippy was going to have a harder time winning over Sweets than Crabs the cat.

While the loaf cooled, Sweets handed Gina a whisk and she dutifully stirred up a milk mixture as it heated on the stove.

"Just until it comes to a slow boil," Sweets said.

"What is it going to be?"

"Butterscotch pudding. I won't have any of course, since Oscar and I are watching our sugar, but it's Cal's favorite."

"I thought he only ate egg whites and bean sprouts."

"Well no wonder he's in a slump," Sweets said.

"Do you watch all his games?"

"Of course. We pray him through wins and losses, Oscar and me." She stopped, wiping her hands on a dishtowel. "Sometimes I think the winning is harder on him."

"What do you mean?"

"The fans. When he wins, they treat him like some sort of hero. They worship him. It's not good for a man to be worshipped." She sprinkled a slow cascade of sugar into Gina's warming saucepan. "I mean forty thousand fans holding up signs, screaming Cal's name, begging for autographs all because he plays a game. Then what happens when he doesn't play well? He's the bum, the rat who made the Falcons lose their shot at the series like last season." She shook her head. "Horrible."

"That's a lot of pressure," she agreed.

"He doesn't need worship; that's for God." She sent a sideways look at Gina. "He needs love."

"I'm not . . ." she started.

"Not what?"

"I don't want you to get the wrong idea. I'm just the dog sitter."

"I guess that will have to do for now."

Gina wasn't sure how to answer that, so she didn't. She whisked away until the pudding came to a boil in glistening bubbles.

When the fragrant dessert was poured into bowls to cool, she helped Sweets set the table and called the men to dinner. Tippy perked up. Gina offered her a bowl of kibble sprinkled with a tiny bit of the meatloaf drippings that Sweets had allowed her to siphon from the pan. The dog rolled on her side, back to the bowl. Gina suspected pique, or perhaps Tippy was waiting for Cal.

Cal and Oscar arrived, but it was clear that something had changed. Cal's expression was grim, eyes burning. Whatever he'd found in the study had not pleased him.

Sweets said grace and they started in on the meal.

Cal fingered his glass of iced tea, his plate untouched. "So was my father pressuring Mom to deed the ranch to him?"

Sweets looked startled. "No. He was here to help Meg. I wasn't happy to see him either, but I came to believe he was good for Meg."

"Good for her?" Cal spat. "As if he didn't dump her twenty years ago?" There was fury in his voice.

Oscar put his own glass down with a thump. "Watch yourself, son. You don't talk to your aunt in that tone of voice."

"Yes, sir." Cal looked at his plate, breathing hard, striving for control. He looked up and reached for his aunt's hand, face torn with regret. "I'm sorry, Sweets. I was wrong to take it out on you. I apologize."

She clasped his hand between hers, fingers

116

tiny in his big palm. "I know it's a shock, honey. No one was angrier than I when your father showed up here."

"Did my mom invite him?"

"No," Sweets said. "But they'd been corresponding via e-mail for a while. He started to visit a few times a week and it really did cheer your mother. They talked about old times, better times. She asked him to help get things in order and he agreed."

Cal closed his eyes. "I can't believe this."

Gina knew it was Cal's worst nightmare, to know that the man he despised had been caring for his mother.

"Oscar and I wanted to tell you he'd been visiting, but Meg thought it would upset your pitching."

"My pitching" — Cal heaved out a breath — "was already upset."

Sweets nodded soberly. "Oscar told Meg and me about how sensitive the athletes were when he played for the Yankees."

"Told them about the guys who would freak out if they couldn't find their lucky socks or sleep with their bats." Oscar chuckled. "Baseball players are a nutty bunch."

"So you figured knowing my dad was around would mess up my mojo?"

"We didn't want to risk it," Sweets said. "You were already so tense. We could see it in your face every time you took the mound. Your press interviews were torture. You could hardly get through them."

Cal flinched, gently removed his hand, and let out a deep sigh. "And I wasn't coming home enough to check things out on my own. I should have been here more."

The recriminating set to his mouth grieved Gina. *Oh, Cal. I know how hard it is to lose someone you love.*

"You were playing your game." Sweets said it in earnest.

Cal looked at her, and his face cracked into a rueful smile. "You sound like Gina."

Gina giggled. "But Sweets probably knows how many innings there are," she said, relieved that the tension had temporarily lifted.

He smiled, and she felt as if she'd won a small victory.

"Dinner's getting cold," Sweets said. "Cal, if you don't eat that meatloaf, I'm liable to sink into a depression and pack myself off to live in the wilderness."

"Better eat it then." Oscar tucked the napkin in his lap. "I'm gonna miss my recliner if we're moving to the wilderness."

Cal picked up his fork and took a bite. A look of bliss crept across his features. He groaned in pleasure. Gina was glad Luz wasn't there to witness it. Egg whites and bean sprouts could never elicit such a reaction.

Sweets could not hide her delight. "Not bad for a two-bit singer."

"Nothing two-bit about you, honey," Oscar said. He turned to Gina. "This gal was a singer with a six-piece band when I was running a ranch in Colorado. Did a dinner show every night at the hotel. Boy, did I eat my share of grub there just to see this looker right here."

Sweets waved a hand. "And I thought you came for the pork chops."

"No way," he said, "But I did have to put away a lot of pork chops before you agreed to see me."

Gina was enthralled by the easy love between Oscar and Sweets. The perfect match, yet they were from such different worlds — a ranch hand and a singer. Like a lawyer and a substitute teacher? Maybe her world and Bill's were not different enough. Certainly God had taken away something she'd thought was meant to be. In spite of the somber thoughts, her stomach rumbled.

She ate her meatloaf and roasted potatoes, relishing both the food and the company.

"So," Sweets said after a while. "You're going to sell the ranch, Cal?"

"Lawyers are telling me to. I can't expect Oscar to keep it up. It's too much for one man."

"Especially a blind man," Oscar put in.

"For any man," Cal said firmly.

Gina had noted that the guest house needed painting and the old water tank in the distance showed signs of rust.

"Place is falling apart," Cal said. "The more I wait, the harder it will be to sell it."

"Could pay people to run it," Oscar said.

Cal shook his head. "Strangers. I'd rather sell the ranch than have strangers running it. Besides, Sweets is entitled to the money from the sale. It was her papa's ranch, too."

Oscar's face hardened. "Don't need the money. Meg deeded that property to you. Not going to take handouts."

Gina could see that Oscar was a proud man. She understood. She had declined her mother's offer of a generous "gift" after she'd lost her teaching position. *I'm not a doctor, Mom, but I can take care of myself, at least.*

"We can talk about it later. What was the favor you wanted to ask me about, Uncle Oscar?" Cal said.

Oscar smiled. "Well, son, I need you to pitch."

"Pitch for whom?"

"Got a team of kids I'm helping out, see, and we need a pitcher for the game tomorrow 'cuz our regular guy is on a cross-country road trip."

Cal squirmed. "Usually when I do these things, it turns into a distraction."

Gina nodded, thinking of the crowd they'd attracted at the fast food restaurant.

"You don't need to worry about that, I promise," Oscar said. "These kids aren't going to be blinded by your reputation."

"What about their parents?"

"How'd you get to be such a cynic, son?"

"The price of fame."

"Remember when you were a kid and I taught you how to pitch? Remember how we used to set up the bottles on the fence and see if you could throw 'em down?"

Cal laughed. "Yes, sir, I do."

"It was fun, right?"

"Yes, sir."

"Well this is gonna be just like that. Fun."

"You guarantee it?"

He forked up a last mouthful of meatloaf. "Be ready at nine tomorrow morning. Gina, we would be honored to have you and Tippy come along too."

"Since you're promising fun, I'm in." She was pleased to see that Cal was not only eating, but devouring his dinner with gusto.

After the meatloaf was gone and the creamy pudding finished, Oscar carried his plate to the sink and Sweets followed up with the service platter. Cal insisted on doing the dishes. Gina grabbed the towel. "I'll dry."

Oscar yawned. "Well, if you all are gonna do KP, I'm going to take my bride home."

Sweets laughed and kissed him on the cheek. "That sounds good, but why don't you let me drive?" she teased.

"Whatever makes you happy," Oscar said.

Sweets and Oscar left, doling out hugs before they did so. Cal helped his aunt into the truck, and he and Gina stood on the porch until they'd driven out of sight. They returned to the sink and Cal dove in to the washing.

"Your uncle and aunt are wonderful people."

Cal scrubbed and handed her a dish. "Yes, they are. I'm lucky."

"Blessed," Gina said automatically.

He continued to scrub, swirling the soapy water, but he did not correct her. She wanted to ask about his father, how he was dealing with the revelation that his absentee parent had been visiting throughout his mother's long illness. How would she feel? She couldn't imagine. They remained silent except for the swish of water and the clink of dishes returning to their homes on the warped kitchen shelf.

Gina took the last plate, dried it, and put it in the cupboard. She heard a smacking sound.

Tippy was dancing around a small square of meatloaf that Sweets must have placed on a paper towel near the spurned kibble.

"I guess Sweets likes Tippy more than she lets on," Gina said.

Cal shook his head at the sight. "Why don't you just eat it, you crazy dog? What's the matter with you?"

Gina offered a pleading look.

"Seriously?" Cal said.

"You don't want her to pack herself off to the wilderness, do you?"

"Actually . . ." Cal said.

Gina threw a dishtowel at him which he caught easily. Lowering himself to the floor, he crossed his long legs and rested his chin on his hand.

Her world set right, Tippy began to wolf down the meal, kibble, meatloaf, and all.

NINE

The next morning Gina hauled herself from bed at just after eight, pulling on jeans and a comfy sweater patterned with green leaves and tiny pink hearts. Securing her hair into a loose ponytail, she stopped at the door of Meg's room. Tippy had stayed up pacing and whining until Gina finally relented and let the dog sleep in Meg's room. She was still there, snoring softly on Meg's bed. Tippy opened an eye. She didn't move a muscle, but her tail whacked against the mattress as if pulled by an invisible string. Tails were an amazing barometer of canine emotions. It would be so much easier if people were as easy to read.

Gina managed to lead Tippy into the kitchen and offer kibble and broth, which Tippy refused until Cal hustled in wearing jeans and a flannel shirt. With his unshaven chin and his baseball cap shoved into his back pocket, he could just as easily be a local rancher as an elite sports star. She liked the look. It suited him.

"Morning. Want some breakfast?" he said.

"To be honest, I was going to sneak out here and eat the leftover pudding for breakfast."

He raised an eyebrow. "Pudding isn't breakfast food."

She shrugged. "It's got milk and eggs. That's close enough."

"I'll scramble some eggs," he said with a smile, going for a pan.

"Can I have mine with the yolks still in?"

He chuckled. "Yeah. Let's throw caution to the wind."

Tippy approached, bonking her head playfully into Cal's shins, paws clickety clacking while she did a good morning jig.

He scooted her to the side with his foot. When the eggs were ready, he handed Gina a plate and mechanically sat down on the floor next to Tippy, balancing his meal on his knee. Smiling, Gina joined him on the floor and the three scarfed up their scrambled eggs and then loaded up in the car, Tippy installed on Gina's lap.

Sweets drove up, Oscar in the passenger seat, and they fell in behind, following the road down the mountain through the minuscule town of Six Peaks, which boasted a post office the size of Mrs. Filipski's kitchen and a doughnut shop, among its other attractions.

They pulled up at an old warehouse which read *Foley's Grain and Feed* on the side in faded letters. Cal peered around. "Oscar must be lost or something."

But Oscar and Sweets got out of their truck.

"Where's the ballfield?" Cal called.

Oscar pulled a bag from the back. "Not ready for that yet. They're just beginners."

"Well, where are we going to play? Got batting cages inside?"

"You'll see." Oscar let the way.

Following a bewildered Cal, Gina clipped Tippy onto a leash and they entered the warehouse. Oscar flipped on the lights, which took several seconds to flicker to life. The warehouse was empty except for a section of fake turf affixed to the floor and surrounded by a standing mesh fence. White lines marked out a home plate and there was another white lined spot for the pitcher. Two blue foam-covered posts stood where first and third bases would normally be.

In a few minutes, the door opened again and people began to stream in, parents toting folding camp chairs and accompanied by girls and boys in the seven- to ten-year-old range, Gina estimated. Some held their parents' hands. Other scooted in using canes to find their way along.

Tippy barked.

"You see, Cal? I told you they wouldn't be blinded by your fame." Oscar smirked.

"Uncle Oscar," Cal said, voice low. "What exactly is going on here?"

"We're going to teach these kids how to play ball, just like when I taught you."

"But . . ." Cal surveyed the group, which had grown to eight strong. "They're . . ."

"Blind," Oscar said. "Got a problem with that?"

Cal looked to Gina as if she might hold the clue to his understanding. She shrugged.

"No, sir, it's just that I don't really understand how we're going to play baseball, you know, with people who can't see."

"You will." Oscar whistled. "Everyone over here now. I'm gonna introduce our pitcher for today."

Sweets helped herd the children toward the makeshift baseball diamond.

Tippy wagged her tail hard as a little boy approached. "Dad, I heard a dog. Where is it?" he said.

"Mark's got a thing for dogs," the dad said. "Is it okay for him to pet it?"

"Her," Gina said. "Her name is Tippy."

127

She crouched and took the boy's hand, guiding his fingertips to Tippy's silky ears. Tippy wriggled excitedly, and so did the boy. His hair was white blond, so much like Matthew's, skin freckled, and eyelashes so fair they were almost invisible.

"I'm Gina," she said. "And this is Tippy. What grade are you in?"

"First grade," he answered proudly. "And I'm on the team. We're the Hornets. Know what a hornet is?"

"Yes, I do. A bug that flies and stings."

"Yeah," he said, laughing as Tippy licked his face. "Flies fast and stings real hard."

Mark's dad was staring at the mound. "The pitcher. Is that . . . ?"

"Cal Crawford," Gina confirmed. "He's helping out Uncle Oscar today."

"Wow. I sure didn't know that. I heard Cal was a relative, but I never expected to meet him." His eyes narrowed and he looked around. "Is this going to be some sort of publicity event? We weren't told about that. We thought it was all about the kids today."

"It's no publicity op," Gina hastened to explain. She was going to add how Cal was at the ranch, preparing it for sale, but then she remembered what had happened the last time she shared too much information.

"He's just here to help."

The man still wore a bemused look as he ushered Mark over to the group. Gina gathered Tippy and moved closer. Uncle Oscar stepped to the mound.

"All right, kids. We've been practicing our fielding and hitting, and today my boy Cal is gonna pitch for us. He knows a lot about pitching, but you can help him with his batting." Oscar grinned. "Pitchers aren't such hot stuff at batting. He's been trying to hit a home run his whole life." Oscar patted Cal's shoulder. "Go meet the kids, son."

Cal looked stricken. "Uh, hey," he said. "Happy to be here." He looked around the circle. "How about we do a high five?" he suggested, wide-eyed.

The kids immediately held up a hand and Cal traversed the circle, delivering high fives to the kids and parents.

"Tell 'em about what you do, son," Oscar said.

"Well . . . I'm a pitcher for the Falcons baseball team," Cal said. "I learned to play from my Uncle Oscar and then I joined a team. Every team has to have a pitcher." Cal continued on, warming to the subject, discussing some of the finer points of baseball. Mark scooted away from the group.

"Where's the dog?" he whispered to his father.

Tippy jingled her collar and Mark left the circle of kids to play with her. He was soon joined by a tiny girl named Ruth and two more boys, Ben and Rohan. Tippy sniffed her way through the kids, causing them to burst out into giggles. Soon all the kids had trailed over, jostling to get Tippy's attention. Cal looked at his disbanded group and then at Gina.

She shot him an apologetic look. Tippy, once again, had stolen Cal's thunder.

Instead of irritation on Cal's face, he threw back his head and laughed, brown eyes lit with a glow that made her senses tingle.

Eventually, Gina got the kids into two groups. Uncle Oscar and Sweets, with the help of a few parents, got half the kids lined up in something of a batting order. The other half were sprinkled around, ready to try out their fielding.

Mark was up first, the bat looking huge in his hands. Oscar activated a tiny speaker in the ball which emitted a beeping sound and handed it to Cal.

"Tell 'em 'ready' when you pull back and 'pitch' when you release," Oscar said. "That's how they know when to swing."

Cal took the ball, a little larger than a softball, Gina noted, and crouched down a little.

He said something to Mark which Gina couldn't hear but that made the little boy laugh. "Ready . . ." he said as he drew back his arm. "Pitch!"

Mark swung the bat so hard it almost knocked him over. The ball thunked to the turf. His face fell.

"Don't sweat it, Mark. We're gonna do this, just you and me, okay?" Cal said.

Oscar helped Mark adjust his stance and Cal lobbed him a soft toss. Another swing, another strike. Mark's cheeks grew red.

Mark's dad called encouragement to the boy, helping him through the next few pitches. Still the ball sailed by out of range.

Then Mark let the end of the bat hit the ground and he looked as though he was about to dissolve into tears.

Gina's heart wrenched.

Cal jogged over and put his hand on Mark's shoulder, bending low to whisper something in his ear. After a moment, Mark nodded, rubbed his sleeve across his face, and picked up the bat.

Another pitch, another miss.

"Come on, Mark. Remember what I told you," Cal called.

Gina wanted to tell Cal to ease up, to let Mark walk away and regroup. He was, after all, only a little boy playing a game that was supposed to be fun. Instead Cal called out again.

"Ready," Cal called out, "pitch." This time Mark made contact and the ball flew past the mound, beeping all the while. With Oscar's help, Mark ran toward one of the foam-covered pillars and smacked it with all the enthusiasm of a player making a World Series home run.

The onlookers burst into cheers as the fielders scrambled to find the rolling ball.

One voice shouted louder than the rest. Cal Crawford, his face lit up like a beacon, pumped his fist in the air. Gina's heart skipped a beat to see the joy there, the joy that must have drawn him to baseball in the first place, before all the pressure, and the heartache. The unfettered pleasure of smacking a ball high and hard out into the field, before baseball became the measure of his self-worth.

"Nailed it," Cal shouted.

Mark's smile was ear to ear.

Yes, you did, she thought.

The warehouse gradually warmed with the heat of the day and all the activity. Cal and two of the parents cranked open the big bay door. A delicious breeze wafted along, ruffling Gina's hair as she hopped along after Tippy to keep her off the playing field.

Cal wished he could just watch Gina for a while as she smiled and chatted with the parents and kids. How did she always know what to say? He heard her laughter bubble up as she gave a little girl a hug. They called Cal "a natural" when he pitched. She was a natural with people. It enticed him, fascinated him. It was like she had the sun inside her, energy which pulled him closer and warmed him. He blinked to rid himself of the strange thoughts.

She's just here to help with Tippy and you've got a plane to catch next week. Don't get distracted. Distractions were bad. They kept him from doing his job for the team and his crazy attraction to Gina had the potential to derail him entirely. *Stay away from Gina Palmer,* he ordered himself.

But there she was, skipping over to him, holding out a sleep mask between her slender fingers. "It's your turn."

"For what?"

"The kids want you to try batting. You have to wear a mask so everything is fair."

"Is that a good idea? What if I hurt somebody?"

"You will be gentle and Oscar says you can't hit the broad side of a barn anyway."

"Very funny, and if that's supposed to get my dander up . . ."

"It worked?" She laughed. "Come on, then. It's almost time for lunch and the parents are barbecuing. I don't want to miss my chance at a hot dog."

He took the mask and put it on.

"Bend down. It's twisted in the back."

He bent, as instructed, and he felt her fingers skimming the back of his head, adjusting the strap along his neck and behind his ears. Her touch sent sparks tingling through his nerves. He wanted to capture her hand and feel the softness of her palm next to his cheek, against his lips. With a jerk, he straightened. "It's good."

She took his arm and led him to the plate, giving him the bat and a final pat on the shoulders. "Keep your eye on the ball this time," she advised, and he laughed.

"And you keep your eye on Tippy."

"Yes, Mr. Crawford," she threw over her shoulder.

One of the dads took the mound.

"I gotta say, it's weird to be pitching to Cal Crawford," he said.

"No weirder than me trying to bat with a sleep mask on."

134

"Ready. Pitch." The dad lobbed a pitch and Cal heard the beeping grow louder and louder until it passed him by. Second pitch, third, and he felt the bat make contact, but only a glancing blow.

"You can do it, Mr. Crawford." He recognized Mark's voice. "Let's go Hornets, let's go."

And then all the children were chanting, "Let's go Hornets, let's go."

He'd heard a lot of cheering fans in his day, but Cal thought none of them had ever put as much feeling into it as these little kids. On the fifth pitch he made contact, a gentle tap that sent the ball rolling onto the green. Pulling up the mask with his thumb, he saw the team hopping and scrambling around, getting excited directions from their parents and Uncle Oscar.

He saw the glint of a camera lens.

"Put on your mask and run," Oscar roared.

Cal yanked the mask back on and jogged slowly toward one of the bases which had started to beep, arms outstretched. What kind of confidence did it take for a blind person to full-out run? The thought bewildered him. Tripping over the edge of the base, he sprawled on the astroturf. A wet tongue slurped across his face as he took off the mask. Tippy gave him another congratulatory lick. Then all the kids cheered as the ball was retrieved. Technically, his brain said, it wouldn't have been an out because he made it to the base before the fielders got control of the ball. His heart corrected. It was a victory for the Hornets, who whooped and shouted as Tippy zinged from child to child, adding her own congratulations. The finest play he'd ever not seen. He sat there and grinned.

From his spot on the ground, he looked for Gina. She gave him a double thumbs-up. *What a smile,* he thought. Electric.

"And they say a pitcher can't hit worth a nickel," he muttered to himself.

As he got up, he saw the glint of a camera lens again, only this time he was able to pinpoint that it was coming from the bay door, and it wasn't a parent capturing the moment for their family. This was a professional camera, aimed right at him, held by the hands of Tom Peterson, stalker extraordinaire.

TEN

Cal was on his feet and sprinting for the bay door. He skirted kids and beep balls, Tippy racing right behind him. Peterson was leaping into his van by the time Cal reached the passenger side.

"Give me the camera," Cal shouted through the half open window. The engine revved and Tippy danced away.

Tom gripped the wheel. "No way, Crawford. Gonna get lots of new followers with these photos. Nothing you can do about it."

Cal banged a palm on the locked door. "These are kids, not photo ops."

"So noble, Cal." Peterson's eyes went hard and flat. "You're living the life I was meant to have. The least you can do is share some of the fame."

"Not at the expense of these kids." Cal yanked again on the door handle, but Peterson stomped the gas, forcing a tight turn that made the wheels squeal. Cal's mouth went dry. Tippy stood directly in Peterson's path, tail wagging as she stared at the vehicle that was about to run her down.

"Move, Tippy," Cal hollered.

Tippy remained, tail whipping back and forth, sides heaving with excitement.

Nerves on fire, he leapt forward, but he could not get there fast enough. Wheels squealed and he lost sight of Tippy. The van surged forward. She would be crushed, the old dog. Panic filled him. He stumbled on, though he knew he would not be able to save her. Through the dusty windshield he saw someone run out from the warehouse.

His stomach dropped as Gina darted into the path of the oncoming vehicle.

"Gina," he shouted over the roar of the engine. Then he almost tripped, catching himself before he fell. Plumes of dust filled the air. With a roar and ping of gravel, the van sped away down the dirt road.

He staggered forward, throat thick with fear. Had he heard a bump? A cry? Or was it the pounding of his own heart? Dust swirled in choking clouds before it began to recede.

"Please, God . . ." he said.

Slowly, the billows subsided, inch by inch. Silhouetted by the sunlight Gina stood there clutching Tippy, panting as tears spilled down her face.

He ran to her. "Gina!"

She only cried harder, sobs that wrenched out of her. He scanned for blood, bruises. He saw only a rip at the knee of her jeans, the skin scraped underneath.

"Please," he said, catching her face in his hands. "Please, Gina. Tell me. Are you hurt?"

Green eyes shimmered back at him, so full of life and emotion. He stroked the satin skin of her cheeks, calming her, calming himself. "Are you hurt?" he repeated.

Gulping, she shook her head. "He . . . he almost ran us over." Another swallow. "I only just got Tippy in time."

He pressed his forehead to hers, letting the relief soak in, Tippy wriggling under her arm, poking her cold nose under his chin. They were unhurt, both Gina and Tippy. "I'm sorry, Gina," he whispered. "Oh honey, I'm sorry."

"Why would he do that?" Her lower lip trembled. "Why?"

He pulled them to his chest, Tippy taking the opportunity to nuzzle his ear.

"He's crazy," Cal murmured. "But you're safe. You and Tippy are safe." *Thank You, God.* He held her closer to reassure himself that he spoke the truth, smoothing his hand along her back and shoulders, traveling the length of her silky ponytail.

"Why am I crying?" she sobbed.

"Just the shock of what happened. It's okay. The crying will help you feel better." It was certainly making him feel better to have her tucked in his arms, warm and safe. He wanted to keep her there, he realized, with a sudden lurch of his unreasonable heart. He should let her go, but what kind of man would he be to push away a distraught woman? So warm, so soft.

She cried on his shirt until people began to spill from the warehouse.

"What happened?" Oscar demanded.

"That crazy guy in the van almost ran Gina and Tippy over," Sweets said. "I saw it all through the door."

Oscar's mouth cemented into a tight line. "He's lucky he got out of here when he did."

"Here now." Sweets reached out. "Let me take that annoying dog and you go sit on the bench for a minute, Gina. Take her over there, Cal. Right now. I'm going to get a bottle of cold water and a Band-Aid for her knee."

Cal led her to the bench, arm around her shoulders. She sucked in deep breaths and he dried her tears with the sleeve of his shirt. He wondered what he should say, but since he couldn't decide on anything he stayed quiet, keeping her in his embrace, feeling rather than seeing the tempo of her body slow, her breathing calm.

How close she had been to the front of the bumper. His stomach clenched. Too close.

"Tippy's an okay dog," he finally said. "But I don't want you getting hurt to protect her."

Gina sighed. "I know. It was dumb. But she was just standing there with that silly look on her face and I couldn't let him run her over, could I?" She beamed him an indignant look.

He squeezed. "No, I guess you couldn't, but still . . . you scared me."

"I scared myself. I didn't think I could run so fast. I mean I eat doughnuts and walk dogs. I'm not exactly an athlete."

He could not help pressing a kiss to her temple. "You were today. Champion sprint. Never seen better."

Sweets arrived with a small first aid kit and a bottle of water. "I'm going to have them start serving lunch to get us back on track." She patted Gina's cheek. "I'm so sorry about that nutty man. He'd better not come back because I see the same look on both Oscar and Cal's faces, and both of them know how to use a baseball bat." She shivered as she hustled away.

Cal didn't know what exactly his aunt saw in his expression, but he knew Peterson had better not come within spitting distance of Gina or Tippy. Ever again. Something very close to fury bubbled in his gut. Cal was not a man easily angered. His mother used to say his temper was like Halley's Comet, infrequent but hard to forget. And now, in the space of two days, he'd gotten angrier than he'd been in years. Maybe it was time to sell the ranch. It was stirring up all kinds of emotions, including a warm tug in his heart he didn't understand when he looked at Gina. She was the dog sitter, and not long ago she was ready to throttle him. What had changed?

To cover his confusion, he took a cotton ball from the first aid kit and squirted on some disinfectant while she rolled up the leg of her jeans.

"It's gonna sting."

She held up her chin. "I can take it. I cry a lot, but I'm tough."

"That's true." He dabbed the scrape clean and applied the bandage, carefully smoothing it into place. "Better?"

She nodded. "I feel silly for crying. I

mean, it turned out okay. I can't understand how someone could run over Tippy. How could someone hurt a geriatric dog without a menacing bone in her body?"

"There are some not-so-nice people in the world, Gina."

She bit her lip. "I've never been very good at realizing people have bad intentions. I always assume they mean well. I'm naive. I've got to get more cynical."

He sat back on the bench and offered her the water. "You're you. My mom would say you're just supposed to be the best you God made you to be."

She smiled and he saw one tear glimmering on her cheekbone like a fallen star. "I think I would have liked your mother."

He reached out and brushed the tear away. "She would have liked you, too." He leaned forward, toward the pink perfection of her lips. They would be soft and warm and connect him to this woman who whirled into his life like a wild fast pitch. So close, her eyes were on his, so green. Another inch closer.

What are you doing? his brain screamed. But he could not stop himself. His mouth almost touched hers when she put a hand on his cheek, stopping him. He blinked, disoriented. Of course she was right. *Back off, right now.*

He did, bolting to his feet. "Looks like the hot dogs are ready. Are you hungry?"

She nodded, standing up.

What did she think of his attempted kiss? A friendly gesture? A friend comforting a friend? He swallowed hard, trying to come up with something to say. "Eggs for breakfast and hot dogs for lunch. This isn't exactly the regimen of champions."

"Babe Ruth ate three hot dogs before every game," she said.

Cal's eyes went wide. "How'd you know that?"

"I read it in a book in your room. *Baseball Heroes On and Off the Field.*"

"You're boning up on your baseball knowledge?"

"Yes, and did you know that Pitcher Jim Abbott was born without a right hand and had a ten-season baseball career, including throwing a no-hitter for the New York Yankees?"

Cal was out and out staring now. "I forgot about that one."

"Page ten in *Baseball Brainbenders.* Tippy and I have been studying, but I am a better student than she is because I don't fall asleep mid-chapter." She stood and waved at Sweets, who was calling them over to the picnic table, wincing as she flexed her scraped knee. "Man, those hot dogs smell good. Ready to get one with me?" She stood there in the sunlight, ripped jeans, hair mussed, cheeks still pink from crying.

He found that there was nothing else in the world he would rather do than eat a hot dog with Gina Palmer. *Just keep your kisses to yourself and everything will be okay.* He tucked her arm in his and headed toward lunch.

In spite of the Peterson intrusion, Gina enjoyed tossing beanbags and inflating balloons for the kids to play with while simultaneously keeping Tippy from popping them. She was sorry when the parents began to pack up and load their kids back into their cars in the late afternoon. Tippy was too tired to do much more than snore in her lap on the way back to the ranch, legs twitching as she dreamed about the fun she'd had. Cal was quiet and for that, Gina was grateful. Her stomach still fluttered, not over what had happened with the van, but on the bench, after. Cal had leaned in to kiss her. The idea filled her with a battery of conflicting emotions — tenderness, trepidation, anxiety, and angst. Did she want him to kiss her? Yes. And no. Her attraction and feelings for Cal were definitely growing every moment, but his life was not hers, his world a universe away. She was going to be a teacher, and besides, after Bill, she wasn't in the market for a romance. Was she? Her thoughts bumped along with the ride.

This time, Sweets allowed Cal to grill some steaks, though she insisted on fixing fried potatoes and her top-secret coleslaw recipe to go along with the meal. Cal stuck with the steak and mournfully passed on the coleslaw. Gina had no such reserve and enjoyed every bit of the fare. Cal again abstained from dessert, this time peach ice cream which Sweets procured from their freezer at home.

When the dishes were dried and Sweets and Oscar gone home for the night, Cal sat on the floor while Tippy ate her kibble.

"You know we can't keep this up, right dog?"

But Tippy did not look at all worried about losing her dining companion. He stayed until Tippy had gobbled the food and licked the bowl clean.

They wandered into the parlor, chatting easily about the day. Cal sprawled on the sofa, Tippy jammed against his muscular thigh. Gina settled in the chair next to the sofa and pulled her feet up underneath her.

"Did you know your uncle was coaching a beep ball team?"

"I didn't even know there was such a thing as beep ball. I'm blown away." He chuckled. "Not surprised he's involved. They need a better place to practice, though." He sighed. "Don't suppose Uncle Oscar is going to let me help out with that."

"Because he's proud?"

"Stubborn."

"Almost as stubborn as you?"

He grinned and then it faded away. "Got to get the study packed tomorrow. Almost time to head back to San Francisco."

"Would it help if I finished boxing up your mother's bedroom? There isn't too much left, really. It would be easy for me to do."

He looked out the window. "I should do it."

"I don't think she would've minded if you had help."

His gaze swiveled back to her. "You think so?"

"Yes."

"She has a ton of shoes. I didn't see her in much besides her old boots, but she collected a mess of shoes. I don't know why."

"It's okay. How about I box them and then you could send them out for donation, or keep them for a while until you sell the ranch."

"You'd do that for me?"

She nodded.

"Why?"

Such a soft syllable, tender and longing.

"Because we're friends."

Now it was his turn to give her a wondering nod, brown eyes quizzical. "I thought I was a heartless egomaniac."

"I thought you were too, but I've reconsidered." She was not sure exactly how the shift had come about. Was it the moment when he had not been able to leave Tippy at the pound? The way he'd treated the children at the beep ball game? Tried to comfort her after the van incident? Or all the up and down moments in between?

He reached for her hand and grazed her knuckles with his lips. Then he rested his cheek there, his stubble tickling her fingers. "Thank you," he said, in a voice so low she almost didn't hear. "I don't deserve a friend like that."

"You're welcome," she said. She allowed him to keep her hand there for a moment, before she remembered. He was a man, a famous athlete, dealing with pressures and stresses she could not hope to understand. She would serve him as an employer, support him as a friend, but that was all. Her heart had too recently been flayed open to allow for anything else. *Remember Gina? Not in the market for a romance.* Gently, she pulled away.

"I'm going to fill up Tippy's water bowl in case she gets thirsty tonight."

He nodded, watching her go.

Her knee stung as she bent to replace the filled bowl. She remembered the feel of Cal's forehead pressed against hers, the tingle of his touch on her face and the worry in his eyes.

Was that the touch of a friend?

Yes, she decided. A friend.

Oh, honey, I'm sorry. She'd heard that before. Recently.

She walked to the parlor to say goodnight and found Cal asleep, one arm thrown over his head as if he was winding up for a pitch. The lamplight blurred out the bruises and the blackened eye, gentled his mouth and the worry lines on his forehead. Tippy was curled up on his stomach now, eyes closed, snoring softly. She could not resist. Gently she leaned over and pressed her lips to Cal's forehead. One kiss. That was all.

Tiptoeing, she pulled a blanket over them both and turned out the light before she left.

ELEVEN

He packed with stoic determination. Files for the lawyers ready to be faxed in one stack. A box of trinkets, Mom's Bibles, a pair of fuzzy green socks and framed photos in the other. He approached it like a pitch, mechanical, precise, no room for emotion, a job to be done. Sweets and Oscar stopped by to help and fix breakfast, both of which he politely declined.

"You're going to be too skinny to throw a fit, much less a baseball," Sweets said. "I'm leaving you a meatloaf sandwich in the fridge for your lunch."

He thanked her and soldiered on.

His cell rang at a little after one, as he finished the last bite of meatloaf sandwich.

"Are you still at the ranch?" Pete said, skipping the customary pleasantries.

"Yeah. Are you going to let me . . . ?"

"No," Pete said, cutting him off. "You're still not pitching until the docs have checked you out."

Cal huffed. "Why are you calling then?"

"You haven't been online recently?"

He looked up to find Gina standing in the doorway, eyes wide, holding up her phone and pointing. "I haven't been looking. Why?" He took the phone from Gina and glanced at the pictures. There he was again, the subject of a trending Tweet, this time the photo capturing him on his back after sliding into the beep ball goal, Tippy slurping him under the chin. Tom Peterson had made good on his word.

He groaned.

"It's been retweeted over ten thousand times," Pete said. "You and Tippy are a sensation."

Cal could hear the laughter in Pete's voice. He could not find words. It was official. He was now the laughingstock of Major League Baseball.

Gina was mouthing something.

"What?"

"The comments are really nice," she whispered. "And you're smiling and everything."

Swell. Now Pete was outright laughing into the phone. "Skipper said he didn't think you knew how to smile."

"I'm glad to be the source of all this

amusement. You called to laugh at me then?"

Gina must have realized the call wasn't going well because she stepped back out into the hallway.

"Not at you, with you," Pete said, "and to tell you to bring Tippy along to Scottsdale next week."

Cal shook his head. He'd heard wrong, or he was actually dreaming the whole scenario. "What did you say?"

"You heard me. The PR people think Tippy is just the thing to draw a crowd to spring training."

"Pete, listen carefully. I am not putting that dog on a plane and taking her to training camp."

"Fine. Then have Gina come and bring the dog. Gina's easier on the eyes anyway. You need all the positive press you can get and the fans want to see Tippy. You'll do some meet and greets together. Let the kids pet the dog while you sign autographs. It will be a hoot."

"But . . ."

"See you when you get back into town."

"But . . ." He found he was talking to no one. Had he really been ordered to bring the nutty dog to training camp? Could they make him do that?

Gina stood hesitantly in the doorway. "Umm, I've mostly finished packing the bedroom." She paused. "I'll just . . . come back later and you can tell me how you want the boxes sorted out."

He let her go.

Spring training was his chance to regroup, to reestablish himself as the best pitcher in Major League Baseball. It was time to put his redemption in action. Was he expected to bring two of the biggest possible distractions along with him for the sake of some publicity shots? No, he decided. He would not comply. There was nothing in his contract that said he was required to make appearances with an animal. And as for Gina . . . he felt again the satin of her skin on his fingertips, the delicious tension in his gut whenever she beamed that smile on him.

That was one distraction he definitely couldn't afford.

Time to go. Time to pitch. The feeling burned through his body. He didn't know how Gina had become his friend, didn't understand why his mother had invited his father back into her life. He couldn't control the actions of stalker Tom Peterson. He could do precisely nothing except pack up the ranch and get back to the mound. Without Tippy and Gina.

Resolutely, he finished the packing.

Time to play ball.

Though Gina wouldn't tell Cal, she followed the Tweet stream all afternoon while she packed Meg's bedroom. To her mind the picture was adorable, a smiling Cal, an exuberant Tippy. Tom Peterson had also Tweeted pictures of Cal pitching to the kids and Gina surrounded by a gaggle of giggling children. Most of the commenters seemed to agree — except for the odd hateful one which she was coming to learn was the inevitable dark part of social media. She was certain Tom was making money off his ill-gotten gains somehow. He had already attracted hundreds more followers with his exclusive pictures of Cal Crawford.

At least it seemed to be helping Cal's public image for a change, though she hoped the parents of the beep ball players weren't too upset at the unsought publicity for their kids.

Gina finished folding the remaining scarves she'd found hanging in the back of the closet. She wondered if Cal's father had packed up the other things, but she didn't want to ask. Cal was upset by whoever had been on the phone, and the Twitter thing had exasperated him further. Best let sleeping dogs lie.

Her particular sleeping dog charge perked up when they heard the kitchen door bang. Hopping off the bed, Tippy scuttled down the hall, Gina following. They found Cal on the porch, sorting out some fishing supplies.

"Taking a break. Going to the creek," he said.

"Oh," she said, hoping she didn't sound disappointed that he did not seem eager to include her anymore.

He snapped the tackle box closed and stood, shooting a sideways glance at her. "Want to come?"

"Really? I'd love to," she said quickly before he had a chance to rethink the offer. "Let me get my bag." She turned to dash into the house. "Oh, um, can Tippy come too? I'm afraid to leave her here alone."

His eyes narrowed and he glared at Tippy. Tippy showed her best by turning in a perfect circle and offering an excited yip. He sighed. "Oh, all right, but you're gonna have to take those socks off her."

Gina complied and they headed along the wooded trail, toting fishing poles and a deliriously happy dog who applied her nose to every pine needle and rut along the way. The trail led down between clumps of oaks, leaves dappling the ground — which was dry thanks to an extended period of drought. Then it was a short, steep climb down to a hollow shelf of flat sandstone. It enclosed a pocket of water some fifteen feet across, fed by a burbling creek. Pines and fir trees shaded the spot in some places and along the far bank, scenting the air with the smell of the woods.

Gina breathed in the beauty of the glorious, sun-dappled fishing hole. "Wow," she said. "So this is home."

He smiled and baited his hook with a salmon egg and then reached for hers.

"Got some beautiful rainbow trout here," he said. "I used to catch a mess of them and my mom would fry them up. They were my dad's favorite."

And how little boy Cal must have been splitting with pride to provide his father's favorite meal. Gently, she took the salmon eggs from his hand. "I can do it. Salmon eggs are good but I prefer nightcrawlers. Of course, the dead bait has the scent and trout just can't pass that up, can they?" She relished his openmouth stare.

"Where'd you learn to fish?" he said as she expertly cast her line into the bubbling water.

"Mrs. Filipski."

"The pierogi lady?"

Gina nodded. "And Butch. He's the mail-man on Mrs. Filipski's route. He showed Mrs. Filipski the best fishing hole in all of California, so he says, and now she closes the store early every Wednesday and we all three go fishing."

He grinned as he cast his own line. "You are a woman of many skills."

"Don't I know it," she joked.

"How's Mrs. Filipski getting along without your help?"

"Funny thing, but Butch seems to be helping out before work and on his off days."

"Is there a romance blooming for Mrs. Filipski and Butch?"

Gina shrugged. "I hope so. They get along like peas in a pod, as my Nana used to say." She eyed the bubbles and Tippy, who sniffed, careful to keep her paws far from the water.

They fished until the sun began to sink behind the pine trees. Sitting on the sand-stone, Gina rooted through her bag and pulled out a bowl and kibble, plus two apples, bottled water, and two sprinkle doughnuts. "Thought we might get hungry. Mrs. Filipski never leaves the shop without iced tea and a container full of cheese piero-gis, but this will have to do."

Cal sank down next to her. Tippy wagged and gobbled, happy to have Cal resting nearby. Cal accepted the apple and water and declined the doughnut.

"I see you found The Doughnut Wheel in town?" he said.

"Your aunt took me while you were packing."

He smiled. "Not surprised." The smile faded away as he looked out across the pond, the sparkling water reflected in his eyes. "Gonna be leaving for Arizona in a few days."

She nodded. "What's it like, spring training?"

"Amazing. Great to be back pitching."

"Is there any time for fun?"

"Fun?" He considered. "It's fun to see the guys again. The stadium is small, more intimate, so the fans can get up closer. Kids get autographs and they have events for them and such. Is that what you mean by fun?"

"I think that would qualify."

"Make yourself at home at the house while I'm gone. I'll leave money for whatever you need for Tippy."

"We'll be fine. How long is spring training?"

"Seven weeks give or take, and then the

traveling starts."

She was not sure why the thought of his leaving made her heart sink. Hadn't she known it was coming all along? "I've got my teaching application in all over the place, but if I get a job, I'll still take care of Tippy for sure or make sure Lexi finds someone else."

"Appreciate that."

Tippy flopped down on her side, ears trailing along the sandstone.

Gina let the breeze ruffle her hair. "This is an amazing place. If it were mine, I would have a hard time letting it go."

Cal wanted to deny it but he found he couldn't. "Yeah, I had some good times here, plenty of them, but some really bad ones, too. It was all before my pitching took off. When I'm here, I almost forget that I'm a pitcher and then when I'm pitching, I lose touch with who I was before."

"But maybe the ranch is where you're meant to remember who you are."

"I'm just a pitcher. I throw a ball. My uncle taught me how when I was eight. That's all I am and I'm the best in the world, or I will be again when I get my head on straight."

"You are more than that."

"Not to my dad," Cal blurted out. Gina

saw his cheeks darken and she knew he regretted letting those words loose.

"To the Lord, and to the people who love you. They don't love you because you can throw a changeup."

He quirked a smile. "You've been studying."

She nodded. "God made you Cal Crawford. The world made you a pitcher."

Cal closed his eyes. "I'm mixed up," he said in a small voice.

"It's okay." She took his hand and they sat, listening to the rattle of dried pine needles skittering across the ground. The minutes ticked by and he stayed so silent, eyes closed, that she wondered if he had fallen asleep.

Her phone buzzed and she checked it. Another text from Bill. *Heard about something you might be interested in.*

She shoved the phone back in her pocket and felt Cal looking hard at her. "Who was that?"

"Bill, my former boyfriend. Part of me wishes he wouldn't contact me anymore, now that he's remarrying his ex-wife."

"Part of you?"

"Oh it's not what you think. I don't love Bill anymore." She picked up a pebble and tossed it in the pond near where they had left their fishing lines trailing in the water. It made a satisfying plop. "I . . . I love his son. His name is Matthew. He's five."

"Ah," Cal said. "And when you and Bill broke up, you lost contact with the boy?"

She nodded miserably, swallowing a sudden thickening in her throat. "Except Bill texts me pictures — of Matthew in his baseball uniform, or eating ice cream. I want to look, but I don't want to feel what comes with the pictures."

He took her hand. "That hurts."

"Yes," she whispered. "It's hard to just stop loving someone when they're gone, isn't it?"

"Yes, it is," he said, squeezing.

The words spilled out of her and she felt powerless to stop them. "We weren't meant to be, Bill and me. He's really smart, a lawyer, super business oriented, and he has spreadsheets for everything. His wife is smart too, more of that corporate type. She has matching shoes and handbags and she has someone make perfume for her signature scent. Not exactly a hands-on mom. They divorced. I think Bill wanted me around more for Matthew than because he loved me, but I didn't see that. I never see that kind of thing."

"Do you miss Bill?"

"Sometimes, but mostly I miss Matthew. I understand, though. His mother doesn't want the former girlfriend around. I wouldn't either, and I don't want to stay in Bill's life, but I just can't seem to get Matthew out of my heart. Do you understand?" She looked deep into those brown eyes, and she thought perhaps he did.

His brown eyes caught the light as he nodded.

"I learned a lot from the whole experience."

"Like what?"

She sighed. "That I've got to take care of myself, stand on my own two feet, and that I'm stronger than the pain."

"That's a good lesson to learn."

She nodded. "Shipwrecks are going to happen, my Nana used to say, and that was one of them. It just made me more determined to go after what I need out of life, you know?"

"I know." He reached his other hand free and trailed his fingers through her hair. Tingles exploded through her body. What was this feeling? It must be nerves, because it couldn't be love. She wouldn't let it be, not until she was over Bill and his son, which might take several decades of concerted effort.

A tug on her pole made her scramble to her feet. She grabbed the rod just as it came unwedged from the rocks and skittered toward the water. Cal joined her as she reeled in the line. A trout some ten inches long and beautifully speckled wriggled and bucked on the hook.

Cal let out a whoop and Tippy pranced around the dangling trout. He took a picture with his iPhone of Gina and the fish.

She grabbed the wiggling thing and carefully disentangled the hook from its mouth the way Mrs. Filipski had shown her. "Off you go," she said, tossing the animal back into the pond.

"Why did you do that?" Cal said. "We could have had trout for dinner."

"I didn't want to kill it."

"What? I thought you were a champion fisherman!"

"Fisherwoman, and just because I catch them doesn't mean I have to kill them." She watched with satisfaction, imagining the fish swimming along through the cold, crisp waters of Slip Rock Creek.

"You're a very complicated person, Gina."

"Nope. Simple as can be. I like dogs and fish and doughnuts. That's about all there is to Gina Elizabeth Palmer."

He looked at her for such a long moment

that it sent something skittering through her insides. Shaking his head, Cal gathered up the fishing gear. "Not hardly. You're going to be a great teacher someday."

"Yes, I am."

They headed back to the house, watching the scrub jays hopping about catching the insects that flittered with the coming dusk. Tippy had a go at a moth, which fluttered teasingly, inches from her nose.

"Figure we'll leave early tomorrow," Cal said, "after breakfast. I've got a flight Monday morning."

"Sounds good," Gina said. She wondered how it would feel to putter around the enormous San Francisco home without Cal there. A week ago she hadn't even known him, and now she found he was in her thoughts and prayers almost constantly. How had she let that happen? Walking quicker, she took the final turn to the house.

Tippy stopped, stiffened, and took off, barking madly.

"Wait, Tippy," Gina shouted. Hurrying as best she could with her bag and jacket, she scurried after the dog. Tippy raced on ahead, careening up to the porch steps. Gina finally caught sight of a man standing there, a very thin, very gaunt man with brown eyes.

Tippy jumped at his knees, pawing at his legs until he bent to pet her.

"Hello, dog," he said.

"Hi," Gina said, coming to a panting stop. "I'm Gina. That's Tippy."

"I know," he said, a quirk of a smile tugging at his thin lips.

"Oh, I'm sorry. Are you a neighbor?"

Cal came up behind her with strong, angry strides. "He's not a neighbor."

Gina looked at Cal, his face blazing as he stared down the man on the porch.

"He's my father," Cal said.

TWELVE

Cal's feet were rooted in place, a hot flame roaring through his body as he faced the man he hadn't seen in two decades. His dad was thin, the skin around his eyes saggy along with the jowls under his chin. His scruff of dark hair had receded, leaving a wide expanse of creased forehead. He looked old and shrunken from the strong, tall man he had been in the twenty years since he had driven away from his family. It did not soften Cal's ire.

"What do you want?"

Mitch bent again to caress Tippy. "Thought we could talk."

"You thought wrong. You don't have permission to be here."

Mitch did not react, merely picked up Tippy and rubbed her head. "Your mother said I could come. I was helping her get the place in order."

"Mom's dead," Cal snapped, both pleased

and ashamed to see his father flinch. "This is my ranch now and I'm telling you to leave. You're good at that, remember?"

Mitch glanced at Gina. "I'm sorry you're having to listen to this, miss."

Cal noticed for the first time the stricken look on Gina's face. Her eyes were wide, lips parted, a look of near horror on her face. *Nice, Cal, way to suck her into this nasty scene.* He tried for a deep breath. "What do you want?"

"I left some things here," Mitch said. "I came to collect them. I would have come sooner but I've been away."

"All right," Cal said, throwing open the front door. "Go ahead and get your stuff and then get out." *Just like you did when I was eight years old.*

He nodded and went into the house, making his way to the study, still holding Tippy.

Cal passed Gina. He wanted to apologize, ashamed that she had seen him so close to losing it. It angered him further that his father, a stranger, could undo all Cal's carefully maintained control. Gina offered a solemn nod and remained outside.

Following his father to the study, Cal watched as he took a set of photography books and a Thermos from the bookshelves Cal had not yet cleared. The way he made himself at home in the study infuriated Cal. As if he belonged there . . . as if he hadn't thrown it all away years ago. Had he come back for a share of his mom's estate? Cal knew from the lawyers that his mother had left a small amount to Mitch. Was the man greedy for more?

"Why did you come, anyway?" he blurted out.

"I told you. To pick up these things."

"I mean why were you here all these months? You walked out on Mom and then you come back when she's dying? What gave you the right to do that?"

He turned and looked at Cal. "I loved your mother . . . and you, believe it or not."

Love? Cal almost choked on the word. It was unreal, like a scene from the sappy movies he abhorred. "You know what? I don't believe it. A man who loves his family doesn't get into his car and drive away."

"A weak man does," he said quietly.

Cal waited. "That's it?" he said after a moment. "You're weak? That's the big excuse? Not a revelation to me, Dad. I already knew that."

"I don't expect you to understand."

"Smart of you, because I don't."

Mitch pursed his lips and let out a sigh. "It's important for a man to support his family. If he can't do that, he begins to feel like less of a man. My businesses were failing, first one store and then the other. I'd spent my whole life building them up, pouring my heart and soul into them, but who wants a photo shop when you can print anything you want at home or to an online company? Who cares about how a camera works, a real quality camera, when you can use a phone without any skill whatsoever?" Bitterness etched the words.

"You became obsolete," said Cal. "It happens. Same scenario for video store owners and people who sell eight track tapes."

Mitch's gaze flicked out the window to the overgrown garden. "We came to live on this ranch because your mom inherited the place from her father. Kind of like charity. Your grandfather never thought I was good enough for Meg in the first place."

Grandpa was right about that. "Ranching was honest work, a way to support us while you tried to keep your precious photo store alive. At least it kept us fed and clothed."

"I'm not a ranching man, Cal. Your mother knew that."

For some reason his father's use of his name struck at him. How many nights had he lain awake, longing for his father's return, imagining what he'd say that would glue their family together again? *I'm back, Cal. We're going to be a family again. Leaving you was a mistake.* Words that never came and never would. He blinked back to reality. "Mom didn't expect you to be an expert rancher and neither did I."

"There was just no way. I do cameras. That's all I've ever done. I tried to show you, remember?"

And Cal had had no interest. None. Nothing about the tiny gears and lenses was anywhere near as enticing as running and catching or fishing in the creek. "Yeah, I remember, but I was a kid and you were a parent and your decision to leave doesn't get laid at my doorstep. Or mom's. You left us because you couldn't rise above your failures and you never looked back. You're right. That's weak." He hammered the last words home like ninety-mile-an-hour fastballs.

"I did look back, Cal. Followed every step of your career."

"So you took an interest after I made it in the bigs, huh? Like everyone else?"

"No, I've checked in with your mother since you were a kid."

He felt like he'd been slapped. "Well, why didn't Mom tell me?"

He let out another sigh, heavy and resigned. "Because I became a drunk, Cal, an alcoholic."

He'd known his father had begun to drink more and more before his departure, but he'd certainly not known that. So what? It didn't change a thing.

"I'm sober now, going on five years, but I abandoned you, and your mother saw what it did to you, how much it cost you. She didn't want that to happen again so we both decided it would be better for me not to be involved in your life while I was drinking."

"People overcome their alcoholism. You couldn't swallow your pride and get help? Not even for Mom? Or me?"

He cradled Tippy closer. "I told you, son. I was weak. Inadequacy is like Kryptonite to a man. I was ashamed for you to see your father as a failure."

Disgust welled up in Cal's gut. This man, too weak to parent, too insecure to stand by his wife's side. He couldn't speak.

Mitch's gaze drifted to the calendar with all of Cal's stats written there for each game. "You've certainly made the best of things. Starting pitcher for the Falcons. Best changeup in baseball."

Something like pride shone in Mitch's eyes and it tore at Cal, bittersweet, a pain-filled pleasure. How he'd longed for his father's approval, and how little it meant after all these years.

"Whatever I've done is thanks to Mom. She took me to all those games, sold her mother's antique jewelry to pay for my pitching coaches and equipment. She was the one who was behind me all the way, Mom and Uncle Oscar. You had no part in any of my success. You don't have the right to feel anything about me, pride or disappointment or anything." He knew his voice was rising in volume but he couldn't stop it. "You're not my father. You're nothing to me."

Mitch's mouth tightened. "I suppose you're right, but somehow I feel proud of you anyway."

Cal and his father stared at each other in silence. "If you're finished," Cal said, "it's time for you to go."

Instead of leaving, Mitch walked to the calendar, picked up the pen, and wrote a series of stats in the box for Cal's final game of the season. "Forgot to pencil that one in." Then he walked past Cal and down the hall to the kitchen.

Cal inhaled the scent of his father's aftershave and it shook him with a sense of mingled pain and nostalgia. His dad was leaving again, diminished, weak. It was what

Cal wanted. He wanted his father to hurt like he had hurt, to feel shame, like Cal had felt all the times he had no father by his side like the other boys. He'd been the one to cut his father down this time, with well-deserved blows. But Cal did not feel triumph, only a cold ball in the pit of his stomach.

Cal followed him to the porch where Gina sat, hands clasped behind her, probably trying desperately to avoid hearing the family mess that had just taken place.

Mitch shifted the dog in his arms. "Anyway, thanks for taking care of her." He headed down the walk.

"Where are you taking Mom's dog?" he demanded.

Mitch turned, giving him a quizzical look. "Tippy is my dog," he said. "I'm taking her home."

Gina jerked, wondering if she had misheard. "Tippy is yours?"

He nodded. "Brought her with me when I was helping Meg. Meg got such a kick out of her that I let her stay, though it really steamed Sweets. Tippy gave Meg something to focus on besides her illness, so I gave Tippy to her with the understanding that I'd take her back after . . ." He cleared his throat. "That she'd return to me. I've been meaning to come sooner and get her, but I was moving places so I figured she'd be okay here at the ranch with Oscar and Sweets for a while."

Cal's eyes were wide. He folded his arms and looked at the ground.

"Well," Gina said through a clog in her throat, "she's a wonderful dog, Mr. Crawford. I sure have enjoyed taking care of her in San Francisco."

Mitch looked surprised. "I didn't know she'd left the ranch."

"I guess you don't go on Twitter."

"What's Twitter?"

Gina was not sure if it was proper in light of the angry words she'd heard spilling from the study, but she pulled the pictures of Tippy and Cal up on her phone and showed them to Mitch.

He chuckled. "Imagine that. Old dog has her moment to shine. Meg would have been delighted."

"People love Tippy."

"I know Meg did, and that dog loved her better than I ever could. All right, Tip. Let's go home." Mitch put Tippy down and said goodbye, walking along the road to where she saw a parked sedan. Tippy trotted after him, but after a few feet she stopped and turned around, scurrying back to Gina and Cal, zinging from person to person and pawing at their legs.

"I'm sorry, Tippy," Gina said through the clog in her throat. "You've got to go with Mitch and we can't come."

Cal did not say a word, nor did he look at the dog.

Mitch called again and Tippy beamed those filmy eyes on Gina. She sank to her knees and kissed Tippy on the head, trying valiantly not to cry.

"I'll miss you, sweetums." She pulled two pairs of socks from her pocket and gave them to Mitch. "It's easier for her on slippery floors if she wears these."

With an amused look on his face, he took them and thanked her.

Tippy sat down and let out a howl.

Gina's floodgates broke. With the hot tears threatening to spill over, she turned away and walked back to Cal. *Gotta say goodbye. You knew it was just a temporary job. Man up.* Tippy tried to run to her, but Mitch scooped her up.

When Gina drew even with Cal, he reached an arm around her shoulders. She ducked her head, allowing the hair to screen her emotions from him, biting on her knuckle. The last thing he needed was a hysterical dog sitter. Cal gripped her tight next to him as they watched. Did the rigidity in his fingers mean he too was sad to see Tippy go?

Mitch opened the door to his car and prepared to load Tippy aboard.

Gina forced out some cheer. "Bye, Tippy. Love you." Too bad her voice broke over the last syllable.

Cal released her, took a step forward, and called to his father. "Wait."

Mitch stopped.

"The team wants Tippy to come to spring training," Cal said. "They want Gina to bring her and do some photo ops and such."

Gina stared. Spring training? What was he talking about?

Mitch considered, looking from Tippy to Cal.

"Is that what you want, Cal?" he asked.

She heard Cal swallow hard and straighten. He looked his father in the eyes. "Yes. I would like Gina to bring Tippy. I'll have Tippy returned to you in a few weeks."

Mitch scratched the back of his neck. "All right, then. I guess Tippy could use a spring training vacation." He stepped back and Tippy rushed toward Gina. Though she knew it was only a temporary reunion, she gathered up the dog and rubbed her cheek on Tippy's head.

She felt Mitch gazing at her. "Thank you, Mr. Crawford."

He gave her a smile and a nod. "There's just something about Tippy," he said. "Meg fell head over heels for her, too."

Then he got in his car and drove away, Cal watching.

"What is this about spring training?" she said, laughing as Tippy licked her ear.

"Gonna have to discuss that, but it's true, they want Tippy at spring training for a week."

They returned to the house and Cal held the door for her as she passed.

Tippy was wanted at spring training?

Gina snuggled the dog close, thrilled to be given a few more weeks with the zany animal. Mitch was right. There was just something about Tippy.

THIRTEEN

Gina was sorry to say goodbye to Sweets and Oscar after breakfast the next morning. They were sent off with cheerful waves and a big pancake breakfast. Cal explained more about Tippy's upcoming adventure as they drove.

"I should have asked you first, before I told my father," he said. "It just sort of came out."

It had, and she thought perhaps there was something else at play. "I thought you didn't want any distractions at training camp."

He shrugged. "It would be more of a distraction knowing that you and Tippy weren't together."

She did not know what to make of that. Had he agreed to the spring training thing so she would have more time with Tippy? Was he that concerned about her happiness? Surely not. Baseball was his life, and spring training, the starting line.

"Are you going to be sad when you have to return Tippy to your father?"

He squirmed on the seat. "I don't want to have anything to do with my father, but if Tippy is his, then that's the way it has to be. Funny, a week ago I would have been happy to hand her over to anyone."

"I wonder how Tippy will react when she returns to him after such a long break."

Cal's face darkened. "Tippy isn't too selective. She likes everyone. I'm sure it will work out. Dad's life always does."

She didn't give voice to her disagreement. Mitch Crawford did not seem like the happiest of men. He'd obviously loved his wife and she knew deep down he must love his son. And now, he had neither in his life. She made a note to add Mitch to her prayer list. The man needed some comfort as much as his son, though she'd never tell Cal that.

They did not stop for lunch and after waiting patiently through massive traffic, they arrived back in San Francisco. He dropped her off at the curb next to the pierogi store. "Tell Mrs. Filipski I apologize about the trip," he called through the window. "If it leaves her shorthanded maybe I can help find someone to fill in."

"Do you know a lot of pierogi makers?"

He smiled. "I didn't even know what a

pierogi was until you told me, but I'm sure Luz could master it. She went to the Cordon Bleu. It's the top-ranked culinary school in the world."

She raised an eyebrow. "You had to look that up, didn't you?"

"Yeah," he admitted. "I never heard of it until I met Luz, but she's pretty proud of it. It's sort of like All Stars for cooks, I guess."

Gina laughed. "Well, if Luz could whip up some pierogis, it would be a good change from egg whites and spinach."

"I don't think my nutritionist would agree."

"Your nutritionist probably does not get asked to bring dishes to the potluck parties."

The light began to fade and streetlights went on. The road was quiet except for the rumble of a city bus making its way along. "So I'll arrange the flight for you and Tippy, okay? There's a couple of events the first few days and then things quiet down and we'll book your flight home."

She shook her head. "We're going to have to drive."

"Flying's a lot faster."

"Yes, but there's the plummeting to earth in a fiery ball of carnage factor."

He quirked a smile. "You're afraid to fly?"

"Not afraid, exactly. I just like having cup holders within easy reach. Besides, Tippy might need to stop and reconnoiter."

He laughed, loud and heartily. "Right. I'll touch base with you tomorrow, okay?"

She nodded, reaching through the window to give Tippy a scratch under her saggy chin. Cal caught Gina's hand, fingers gentle on her wrist, pressing a quick kiss to her knuckles and sending a path of heat up her arm.

"I'm sorry about that scene with my father. It was wrong to unroll all that in front of you."

"That's okay. It caught you by surprise."

"Took my eye off the ball." He sighed. "I've been doing that a lot lately. Should have known my dad was sniffing around at the ranch."

At your mother's request. She thought perhaps it was more helping than sniffing, but she didn't say so.

"I'll talk to you soon," he said.

He let go of her wrist and she waved as he and Tippy drove away. She turned to find Mrs. Filipski and Butch watching out the window. They both broke into frenzied dish-washing when they realized Gina was on to their spying. She stuck her head into the kitchen and offered to help with the dishes.

"No need," Mrs. Filipski said. "Almost done."

"I've got to talk to you about another trip I have to take," Gina said, "but Cal said he can send a replacement to help while I'm gone."

"You take your trip. I've got enough help around here."

Indeed Mrs. Filipski looked very comfortable working next to Butch, who did not seem to mind wearing the floral-patterned apron she'd loaned him. Gina smiled inwardly. Who would think the mailman would be a match for the crusty Polish pierogi maker? The Lord had made stranger matches. Butch offered a soapy salute and continued to scrub.

"Thank you, Mrs. Filipski. You're the best."

"Don't I know it. There was a note left under the mat for you. I stuck the paper on your bed. You want something to eat? I got leftover cheese pierogis in the fridge."

"No thanks. I'm just tired out and ready for bed."

"Yeah? What did you do at the ranch? Milk the cows? Feed the chickens?" She laughed at her joke.

What had she done at the ranch? Learned to play baseball for the blind. Caught a fish and let it go free. Met the people who made Cal the compassionate man he was deep inside and the father who'd let him down more profoundly than he'd ever admit. She'd packed up a beloved mother's belongings while Cal had stowed away his memories and made plans to sell the ranch. And they'd both seen Tippy try to make canine sense of the present and the past, to decide between strange humans who must possess a thing to love it.

What had Gina done at the ranch? Too much for her to make sense of at the moment. "I'll tell you all about it later," she promised.

Heaving herself up the stairs, she made it to her tiny bedroom. Turning on the bedside lamp, she flopped backward onto the mattress, letting the past few days wash over her again. She remembered the feeling of Cal's fingers trailing through her hair, the admiration on his face when she'd caught the fish, the way he'd held her when she'd almost been run down by Tom Peterson. There had been such deep emotion in his face, in his hands. Fear? Compassion? Something more?

Her heart thunked at the memories and the cascade of feelings they awakened inside her. It had been easier when she'd believed

Cal to be a coldhearted egotist who would consign a dog to the pound without a backward glance. Now she had the distinct impression he'd been relieved to keep Tippy around for another week, and not just because she was requested by the Falcons organization.

Another week. A matter of days and it would be all over. After spring training Tippy would go back to Mitch and both Cal and Tippy would disappear. She threw a hand over her eyes and her forearm brushed a piece of paper. She sat up and held the paper to the light.

Gina, I stopped by to see you since I didn't hear back. Did you lose your phone again? You have to get a locator app on that thing. Got a lead on a job for you at Mt. Olive. Matthew has been asking to go get ice cream with you, like old times. Call me. Bill

A job. At Mt. Olive. She read it twice and tried to figure out all the angles. Bill felt guilty, no doubt, about how things had gone between them. He was being kind, offering to help her find a new position. Getting a shot at a potential classroom assignment made her prickle all over. But calling Bill? Hearing about Matthew straight from his father's mouth? Enduring the pleasantries as if they were only friends and she hadn't come to love his son? Sharing an ice cream and watching him walk away again? It didn't feel right, though the desire to see Matthew nearly swamped her.

And reopening the connection to Matthew would shred what was left of her heart.

Find your own job, Gina. You don't need someone to make it happen for you. Don't let anyone take care of you.

Resolutely, she pulled up the school district employment page and made sure her applications were all up to date. Free to interview immediately?

Absolutely. Almost. Right after she and Tippy took a little spring training road trip.

Mind settled, at least for the moment, Gina headed toward sleep, thinking she had better be careful not to leave the car keys within snatching range during their adventure.

Cal relished the sights and smells of spring training. The intimate field where they did batting practice and would play their games reminded him of the hundreds of fields his mother had carted him to over the years. No matter how far away, how dismal or inhospitable the temperature, his mother endured it all with a smile on her face and a book of crossword puzzles to keep her busy during the inevitable wait times. Beside her was always a bag packed with extra water and snacks "in case anyone forgot to pack some." She'd come to as many of his major league starts as she could. The thought awakened an ache inside him, but he found it was a tolerable ache. Somehow it felt better than the numbing void he'd fallen into.

The Scottsdale Stadium field was a dazzling green, precisely manicured and immaculately tended. As a ranch kid, Cal appreciated the skill and backbreaking effort the groundskeepers put in to keeping the turf perfect. Lon, the head groundskeeper, waited in a discreet corner of the stadium, talking into his radio and fussing over every detail of the immaculate turf. He was invisible to most of the players and all of the fans, but not to Cal. Cal trotted over to see him.

"Field looks amazing, Lon."

Lon did not smile, but Cal could see the flash of pride on his face. "Thank you very much, Mr. Crawford. My guys sure appreciated the pizza lunch you arranged for them."

"Please call me Cal." He shook Lon's hand. "You deserve more than pizza."

"Thank you, Mr. Crawford."

Cal sighed and shook hands one more time. He'd known Lon for going on four years now and he suspected the man would never use his first name. They'd been able to sit and talk about mowers and Lon's passion for his apple orchard at length, but here on the field, it was always Mr. Crawford. He clapped Lon on the back and left him to his radio.

Breathing in, he checked his body for tension or soreness and found there was none. He'd enjoyed the light workout in the Falcons' training facility after he'd won approval from the team doc. Elation twirled through his gut as he headed toward home plate for their first full squad workout.

Julio Aguilera fell in next to him, grinning. "You got your groove back, Boots. Changeup was really breaking this morning."

Cal hid his excitement. His "go to" pitch, the split finger changeup, had been right on the money, starting in the zone and dipping down toward the plate, seemingly defying the laws of physics. Even Ag had a hard time snaring it because of the violent break at the end. It was a pitch he could not control at the end of last season, a pitch that had cost them runs and ultimately the championship. "Yeah. Everything felt right, like it used to back when I started."

Ag scratched his ferocious beard. "Could

be the gals are good for you, man."

"What gals?"

"You know, the dog and the blondie sitter. She's a nice-looking girl. Great smile."

He didn't answer, but quickened his steps. Ag trotted to keep apace.

"Hear she's coming up. When?"

He offered a casual shrug. "Not sure." Actually, he'd been wondering the same thing, checking his phone for texts about her progress. He'd even called once and gotten her voicemail.

No distractions, remember?

They were met on the field by the first baseman, Jean, and Tyler, their impossibly young second baseman. Kid hardly looked old enough to shave, undisguised eagerness written all over him. Cal used to be the young hotshot on the team. When had he been replaced in that category?

"Here's another one," Tyler said, laughing at his cell phone screen while Jean and Ag crowded in to see. "She's at some diner. Hashtag is #Tippysighting. Aww man," he said, laughing so hard Jean grabbed the phone from him. "Dog's wearing those socks. That just kills me."

"What are you talking about?" Cal swiped the phone from Jean. The picture was of Gina holding Tippy, surrounded by a group of diners all holding their dogs. Each and every dog was wearing baby socks and one proud owner of a white fuzzy mutt held a sign that said, "Go Falcons."

"How . . . ?" Cal started.

Tyler wiped his eyes. "Apparently, the owner of the diner has some sort of rescue group. He recognized your girl and Tippy and he called up his people. They started some sort of weird Tippy fan club."

She's not my girl, Cal wanted to say. He found he could only stare at the photo of Gina, a pink knit cap on her head which matched the flush on her cheeks and that smile. Oh, that smile. It surged through him, right to his heart with a feeling better than pitching a perfect game. He shook his head. Nothing was better than pitching a perfect game. His teammates would take him straight to the looney bin for even suggesting it.

Ag nudged him in the ribs. "Good for you, like I said."

Tyler was still laughing as he pointed. "Freddie the Falcon's gonna be mad, though, if Tippy steals his thunder."

Freddy the Falcon was actually played by Harvey, whose last name Cal did not know. Harvey was in the wings, suiting up in his puffy Falcon costume. The guy looked peeved as he zipped up, but then again, wearing a polyester bird suit in Arizona and posing for pictures with twelve thousand fans could make a person cranky. Cal shuddered and offered Harvey a friendly thumbs-up.

Harvey did not return the gesture, stalking off to meet the fans who had begun to trickle in.

Cal fingered the glove tucked under his left arm, a yellow Mizuno with the basket weave webbing to prevent batters from seeing his grip on the ball. He got teased for the color, though he insisted every year on the same style. Though each season required a new glove, they were always yellow Mizunos in honor of the first professional glove Uncle Oscar had given him. He still had that glove in a drawer. He slid his fingers inside the supple leather, encountering something that shouldn't be there.

Peering inside, he extracted a rolled-up piece of paper. It was a printed picture of him lying on his back, fist raised in the air after scoring his first beep ball run, Tippy pouncing on him to help celebrate. There was a note scrawled across the top in magic marker. *Toppled by Tippy.*

He looked up to see Tyler, Ag, and Jean laughing.

"You guys are hilarious, you know that?"

They broke into loud guffaws and he found himself chuckling, too.

"Man, Boots, your dog is getting better press time than you, dude," Ag said.

"Not anymore," Cal said. "I'm here to play ball. You three going to join in or find jobs at the local comedy club?"

They were still laughing as they lined up for a team photo. Making sure that none of the guys would see, Cal carefully folded the picture and stuck it back inside his glove.

Gina waved to the group of giggling teens gathered in front of the coffee shop. She sighed, knowing she and Tippy would be plastered all over the cyber universe in a matter of moments.

"I'm beginning to understand how Elvis must have felt." Tippy lolled in the passenger seat, exhausted from greeting yet another round of fans. "Who would think a dog could reach such realms of stardom?"

Tippy answered with a wide yawn and an ear flap. Gina was tired, deservedly so. Tippy had accompanied her into the ladies' room, carefully tied to the stall handle while Gina took care of business. That proved disastrous when Tippy grabbed the end of the toilet paper roll while Gina was washing her hands and away she dashed, out the door, festooning the dining area with arcs of fluttering white paper. Stopping the gleeful canine required the help of four kindhearted and highly amused patrons while the rest recorded it all on their iPhones.

Relieved to be finishing the last leg of the journey, Gina drove on.

She followed the directions Cal had given her and by evening they were in Scottsdale, checking into a pet-friendly hotel. She followed a beaming manager named Marg who opened the door to a luxury suite.

"Oh gosh," Gina said. "We don't need a king bed. It's just me and Tippy." She peered into the bathroom. "This thing is larger than my whole room in San Francisco."

"Mr. Crawford insisted on our best." She handed Gina a pink box.

Bemused, Gina opened it to find a frosted doughnut with rainbow sprinkles. "We've bought a fresh one every day, not knowing exactly when you'd arrive," Marg said proudly. She also held up a bag of Cheetos. "And these, in case Tippy is being finicky. Mr. Crawford said he was concerned she might be."

Gina was too floored to speak. Cal had thought to provide doughnuts for her and

Cheetos for Tippy? A feeling both tickly and soft filled up her insides. How had she ever thought of him as heartless? She realized she was probably blushing madly.

"Wow. Well, thank you. I sure appreciate all the trouble you went to."

"No trouble at all. You let us know if there's anything we can get for you or Tippy. It sure is an honor to have a famous dog here and all. I saw her on Twitter, dragging that toilet paper all over the restaurant. I never laughed so hard in my life," she said, wiping her eyes. She stopped near the door. "Um, do you think, I mean, I know it's unprofessional, but would you mind if maybe I took a selfie with the two of you? My grandkids would just be over the moon."

"No problem." Gina hoisted the tired dog and they took the picture.

When Marg was gone, she texted Cal. "Here in Arizona. Enjoying my doughnut. So sweet of you."

He texted back immediately. "When are u coming?"

"Be there first thing tomorrow."

"Glad."

He was glad, and she realized that she was very glad, too. The light seemed to shine a little brighter now that she was in the same town as Cal, the spring breeze a bit more delicious. Glad, she decided, thanking God for their safe journey and for the spring training madness that lay ahead. Then she gave Tippy some water and a Cheeto and ate her doughnut, the perfect bedtime snack.

FOURTEEN

The park was abuzz with a BBQ Baseball Meet and Greet. Folks had shelled out a chunk of change to enjoy their burgers and hot dogs, clustered on blankets spread across the green. More than the food, what they wanted was an up close and personal with the players and coaches. As Cal looked on from the tunnel, he braced himself for the onslaught of fans. Freddy the Falcon, aka Harvey, was already hard at work, offering high-fives and photo opportunities to the youngsters.

Ag was working the crowd, accepting the adoration which he relished as much as his wife's pork adobo. The gentle giant bent down on one knee and chatted it up with everyone from grandmas to fathers to the youngest toddlers.

Cal smiled, wishing he was as much at ease for the promo events. He'd never enjoyed the strange dance — people who felt they knew him so well, yet they struggled to make conversation once they were face to face. Really they just wanted pictures to provide proof of the encounter so he tried to accommodate, but he didn't do it nearly as well as Ag. He scanned for Gina, checking his phone again. He was about to send another text when he heard an angry shout. Startled, he saw Freddy the Falcon sprinting down the first base line, inches ahead of a growling, snapping Tippy.

He blinked. Twice. The image in his retinas must be a hallucination. He'd almost convinced himself of it when Gina emerged, running behind, sundress flying and floppy hat clapped to her head with one hand.

"Tippy, noooooooo."

Tippy was closing in on Freddy somewhere in foul territory when he tripped and fell flat on his beak, sending up an angry puff of dirt. Lon the groundskeeper was not going to be pleased with the mussing up of his field. Cal finally overcame his shock, running past the ogling crowd to help.

Tippy pounced on the fallen bird man, snarling and poking with her wet nose, tugging at the loose feathers on his churning ankles.

"Stop, Tippy," Gina hollered, trying to grab her collar. "That is so not nice."

Tippy ignored the command, wrestling with the fowl leg waving vigorously in front of her muzzle. She dove again, barking, this time at the other ankle.

"Tippy, get down," Cal thundered.

Electrified, Tippy sat, one orange feather stuck to her lip, staring at Cal.

Gina looked from Cal to Tippy to Freddy. Without a word she scooped up the dog, plopped her in Cal's arms, and tried to help the fallen falcon.

"Oh, sir. I'm terribly sorry."

Harvey rolled on his back and ripped off his headpiece. "What is the matter with that dog?"

"I have no idea." Gina tried to grab his elbow to help him up, but he shook her off.

Cal added his apology. "Really sorry, Harvey. I think the feathers freaked her out or something."

"A dog like that should be destroyed," he snapped, clambering to his feet.

"She's not usually aggressive," Gina said. "As a matter of fact, I've never seen her aggressive at all. She doesn't even like her chew toys. I'm very sorry."

"It won't happen again. What can I do to make it up to you, man?" Cal said.

Freddy brushed the dust off his feathers. "You just keep that dog out of my way." He

197

donned his headpiece and marched back to the crowd.

Gina's eyes were still round with horror. "I can't believe that just happened."

"Me neither," Cal said.

"What if Tippy goes after a fan? A child?"

"Unless they're wearing a bird suit, I think we're safe."

"It's not funny, Cal."

He tried to wipe off his smile. "You're going to be right there all the time with Tippy. If she acts up, you can give her a timeout or ground her or something."

She took off her hat, dejected. "Some dog sitter. Every time we set foot in a baseball arena something bad happens."

He slung an arm around her and dropped a kiss on her temple. "It's a ballpark, and don't worry about it. No harm, no fowl," he could not resist adding.

She was not amused. "I feel terrible."

"These things happen." He laughed. "Actually, things like this don't happen unless Tippy's around."

"That's not comforting."

Though Cal was sorry for Freddy/Harvey's embarrassment, he felt something else altogether, a mixture of amusement, delight, and something completely different. He gathered Gina in his arms, Tippy and all, and planted another kiss on the top of her head. "Welcome to spring training."

She relaxed in his embrace. With a little sigh that thrilled right through him, she tucked her head under his chin. "How has it been going before Hurricane Tippy arrived?"

"Couldn't be better," he said. "First couple of days were perfect."

Tippy wriggled to be put down, and Gina broke off the embrace, much to Cal's disappointment.

"I'd better keep up with her." Gina headed back to the gathering and he jogged to catch up.

"Pitching is good?" she said.

"Pitching is great."

She gave him a thumbs-up. "We're going to keep out of your way, I promise. No distractions if I can just keep her separated from the mascot. You don't have any other people in animal costumes around, do you?"

"Not as far as I know."

They rejoined the group and immediately a crowd formed around them, jostling for pictures. Harvey the Falcon put his wings on his hips in annoyance. Cal found he did not mind the press op quite as much with Gina and Tippy there. The nutty dog was her usual irrepressible self, unless Freddy the Falcon came near. Then she would curl her lip and snarl, to the delight of the crowd who took pictures to their hearts' content.

Ag hustled over and kissed Gina's hand, which made her laugh.

"So Tippy's arrived to be our new mascot?"

"Oh no," Gina hastened to say. "Just doing a few photos and then the dog and I are going home."

"No rush," Ag said, winking at her. "Why don't you come to the clubhouse tonight? We're just having a few laughs. Wives and kids will be there, so we won't get too out of hand."

"Well . . ." Gina shot Cal a questioning glance.

He usually did not attend the family nights. It always made him melancholy to see the guys there with their ladies, babies and little kids milling around. But why not? Pitching was great today. No need to go over tapes for hours. Maybe it wouldn't hurt to stop by for a while, especially with Gina there to charm the socks off everyone.

"Yeah. Let's do that," he said to her. "I mean, if you're not too tired."

"She's not too tired," Ag said. "Plenty of energy, right?"

Cal surveyed the line of people some

twenty deep, patiently waiting to have their moment with Tippy the dog. "Maybe we should wait and ask her after she makes it through her first meet and greet."

Gina straightened her shoulders and beamed a full kilowatt smile at the first kid in line. "No worries. This is way easier than trying to get them to sit still for a math lesson."

Gina led Tippy to the front of the line and introduced herself.

Ag and Cal looked on.

"Kids would rather meet the dog than us, man," Ag laughed.

"Given the choice, I would, too." Ag punched him playfully in the arm.

Second in line, a towheaded little kid, probably all of five years old and wearing a Falcons jersey, wiggled in anticipation. His father stroked his head indulgently. When the boy got to the front, he wrenched away from his father and threw his arms around Gina.

"Hi, Gina. I missed you," he squealed.

She let out a cry and hugged him, smiling a mile wide. The father embraced her too, in a familiar way that didn't set right with Cal. He edged closer.

"What are you doing here?" he heard Gina say.

"Matthew wanted to see you and you know we're big Falcons fans," the man said.

It must be Bill, the man who'd dumped Gina. Guy looked all right, genial and smiling, well dressed, but Cal knew he was a toad underneath. What was he up to, bringing his kid to visit?

As Gina sank to her knees to gush over the little boy, Bill's gaze swiveled across the field and found Cal. He bobbed his chin in the manly, "We're members of the same species" way.

"We're not," he muttered to himself. Gina continued to beam, chatting with Matthew as Tippy gave him a thorough slurping. Had Gina forgotten that this father had left her with a broken heart? And why, he wondered, did the sight of Bill give Cal a knot in his stomach?

She could see who she wanted. Befriend who she wanted.

Leave when she wanted. Why should he care?

Because he and Gina were friends, and he didn't want to see his friend get hurt again, he told himself.

Bill pointed in Cal's direction.

As Gina began to turn, perhaps to summon Cal to meet this Bill and son, Cal

202

drifted away, a shadow clouding his good cheer.

Gina felt Cal's strong hand on her back, guiding her into the clubhouse. It was furnished with comfortable leather chairs, a massive dining table, and a big screen TV. She still felt unsettled by the sudden appearance of Bill and Matthew, sweet angel Matthew.

"What do you think of the place?" Cal was saying.

"Very nice," she said. "I was imagining something along the lines of the clubhouse my brother built out of scrap wood in the backyard when we were little. I wasn't allowed in since I was a girl, but I snuck in one time and I found out where all the missing snacks from the kitchen had gone."

"Can I get you a drink?" Cal asked. His tone was a little more formal, she thought, though she could not quite see why.

"Lemonade," she said. "Please."

Immediately she was approached by two wives, toting their little boys along. "You must be Gina," the taller one said. "I'm Allie. We've been watching you and Tippy on Twitter."

Gina grimaced. "I don't know how they keep getting these pictures. It's crazy."

"Pro sports is a crazy business." Allie pointed. "Is it okay if Josh pets Tippy?"

"Sure," Gina said.

The second woman introduced herself as Tonya. She was elegant, well dressed with French-tipped nails and a red bag that matched her shoes. Gina felt suddenly aware that her sandals were scuffed and her sundress had been purchased at a thrift store two years before. "So are you and Cal together?" Tonya said.

"Uh, no. I'm his dog sitter."

Allie smiled. "Oh, you're more than that. He can't stop staring at you."

She looked over to find that Cal was indeed watching her while he waited for a server to fill a glass with lemonade. He looked away to check his phone.

"Must be the dog. No one can help staring at Tippy."

Allie laughed as another woman moved to talk to her. "He's not looking at the dog. See you later."

Allie and Josh moved away. Gina took a moment to try and collect herself. Ever since Bill had appeared with Matthew, she felt as if she was unable to get a full breath. Matthew pleaded that she come play catch with him, and it took all her fortitude to decline.

"Soon," Bill told Matthew. "I've got to talk to Gina later and we can play then."

"Don't answer for me," she'd wanted to say, but he was rushing on.

"Are you free tomorrow after breakfast?"

"I'm really not sure what my schedule is," she'd said.

"We'll keep it flexible then," Bill had said, picking up Matthew and wrapping them both in a hug. She'd found herself breathing in the scent of Matthew's shampoo, the kind that came in the blue shark bottle found on the second shelf of the third aisle in Don's Meat and Grocery.

Cal interrupted her thoughts. "Here's your lemonade."

Pete found them next, crushing Gina in a cigar-scented hug and bending over to scratch Tippy.

"How's my girlie?" he asked her.

Tippy flopped over and offered him a tummy to rub.

"You know, I've got my boat all back in order and the missus moved in. If you're still looking for a home for this old bag of bones after spring training, I can take her. Missus will tend to her while we travel. She says it's more fun taking care of a dog than me anyway."

Cal's face darkened. "Appreciate that.

Actually, we found out Tippy didn't belong to my mother."

"Really? Family friend?"

"No. My father."

Pete blinked. "Awww man. So Tippy's going back to your father?"

Cal nodded and Gina felt a pain inside for him and for herself.

Pete considered. "So you . . . talked to your dad then?"

"As little as possible," Cal snapped. "He showed up at the ranch without my permission, and it won't happen again. As a matter of fact, I'm going to sell the place."

"Okay."

Cal rounded on him. "What do you mean, okay? That's the kind of 'okay' you give me when you've got something else to say."

Pete held up his hands. "I got nothin'. Just going to enjoy some chips and guacamole that I'm not supposed to eat, according to my doctor, but I did wanna tell you there was a message in the office for you."

"From whom?"

"Your father, as a matter of fact. He asked you to call. Said he didn't have your cell."

Cal muttered something under his breath while Pete wiggled his fingers at Gina. "See you, Gina."

Gina pretended to fuss with Tippy, but

she shot a look at Cal. He was staring into space, mouth pinched.

"Are you okay?"

"Yeah. Why wouldn't I be?"

"I just wondered. Does it upset you that your father called?"

"No. He can call all he wants but he's not getting any response from me."

Clearly not her business. "Okay."

"I'm going to take Tippy outside for some air. Do you want to come?"

She did, following him out onto a patio. The temperature was warm but not sizzling. Strings of twinkle lights hung over the small tables. Tippy set off to give the walled-in patio a thorough once-over.

Cal sat at the table, fixing his inscrutable brown eyed gaze on Gina. "Saw Bill and Matthew at the meet and greet. That was them, right?"

She nodded, sinking down across from him. "What a surprise that was. Matthew's grown a couple inches since I saw him last." Her heart throbbed when she said his name. "He'll be a first grader soon. He's decided to be a firefighter when he grows up. Or a circus clown." She laughed. "I'm sure Bill's holding out for lawyer."

"What does he want?"

"Who? Bill?" She shrugged. "He brought

Matthew for spring training. He's on a T-ball team. So cute."

"What does Bill want?" Cal's tone was hard.

The smile faded from her face. "With me? I don't know. Probably to tell me about this job he's heard about. Deep down, he really does want to help me."

"You sure?"

She frowned. "Why do you ask that?"

"I've seen that look before. Bill may have other things he's after."

"Like what?"

Cal sat back in his chair and folded his arms. "To get close to me."

Her mouth fell open. "What?"

Cal stayed silent.

"You're saying you think he came to spring training because he's using me to get to you?"

"It happens."

"Because you're so famous and all that."

"Like it or not, yes. I am famous and people are weird about fame, just like I told you before."

She felt a slow burn. "Did it occur to you for one moment that he's fond of me? We shared time together."

"Until he dumped you when his wife came back."

She felt like she'd been slapped. "I'm aware. And I'm also a smart girl, Cal, even if I'm not a very good dog trainer."

"I'm not saying you're not smart."

"I think you are. You think I'm so clueless I wouldn't even recognize that I was being used?"

"You're putting words in my mouth."

There was a loud humming in her ears. "Listen," she said, getting to her feet. "I realize that I'm not of your world. I don't get shuttled around in limos and have the world falling at my feet because they like the way I throw a ball."

"That's not what . . ."

The blood simmered in her veins. "But I did have a life before I came under the shadow of Cal Crawford. People value me because of who I am, not who I work for."

He looked at the table. "It was just a friendly warning."

"Not friendly," she said. "Not really."

"I didn't mean to insult you."

"As a matter of fact, I think you did. And you know what? I got the message. I've been put in my place and reminded of my position in your life. I'm the dog sitter and I must not allow myself to be an avenue of access to my celebrity boss. Don't worry. In a few days, I won't be your employee anymore anyway. That reminds me that I've been neglecting my own goals. Thanks for the lemonade. Come on, Tippy."

In loyal fashion, Tippy scurried over and let Gina affix her leash. They sailed out. Though she listened carefully, Cal made no effort to follow.

Surprisingly, she did not cry. *Better to find out now how he really feels, Gina. In a few days, you'll never see him again.* This time, the end of her employment couldn't come quickly enough.

Cal paced the floor of his room. He had slept no more than a few hours. It was still not yet sunup and he found himself walking to the office adjoining the clubhouse.

A night janitor looked up in surprise. Cal didn't know the guy's name, though he'd been a fixture at the clubhouse for years. Gina would have learned his life story at their first meeting. Thinking about her made his throat feel thick. What had caused him to behave like such a jerk the night before?

. . . he dumped you when his wife came back. Had he really said that? His mother would have skinned him alive to hear him speak to a woman in such a manner. And why had he?

To protect her, to make her wise up about

Bill. She'd said it herself, she was naive, too trusting.

But what was it to him if Bill was using her to get to him? Wanting a piece of the great Cal Crawford?

Great. The word made him think of Gina.

"Maybe when your mom said God made you great, she wasn't talking about your pitching." Gina certainly wouldn't put Cal in the great category now, but he'd definitely qualify for jerk status.

He rubbed a hand over his face, feeling the fatigue hit home. Mentally he inventoried his pitches — cutter, split finger fastball, slider, changeup, curveball. Repeating the list in his mind soothed him. Everything he was in the world came down to his arm and a five-ounce white leather ball. Fingers clenching, he longed for the comfort of a baseball at that moment. That was exactly how he was going to be great, and he wouldn't allow himself to be distracted by anything — not a woman, not his father, not a dippy dog. *Deal with the note and get it over with.*

The janitor stood there sweeping the front walkway, broom in one hand and dustpan in the other. "Hey, Mr. Crawford. What brings you out at this hour?"

"Pete said there was a message left for me

211

in the office. Would you let me in so I can get it?"

"Of course." He unlocked the door, fingers thick and knobby at the knuckles. The back of his head glistened where a bald spot parted the grizzled hair. Guy had probably been doing the job forever, starting as a young man and quietly working his way into old age. He thought of Gina, who knew everyone's names — from the doorman to the gas station attendant.

"Thank you," Cal said.

"Sure thing. I'll lock up again when you're done. Take your time, Mr. Crawford."

"Great." The man held the door for him.

"I should know this, but what's your name, by the way?" Cal asked as he passed.

"Me? Norm. Norm Weston."

"Thank you, Norm, for letting me in and keeping the office so clean. You do a good job."

His eyebrows arched, lifting his sagging face for a moment. "Oh, uh, well . . . thank you, sir."

"I'm sorry to cause you trouble."

"No trouble at all, sir."

Cal nodded and let himself into the office. He found the board where the miscellaneous notes were tacked and removed the one with his name on it.

Cal, from Mitch Crawford.

Mitch Crawford. He still felt a flood of emotions where his would-be father was concerned. The man whose name he bore, who had so little influence on his life. No, strike that. The man had a whole heaping load of influence. When he'd left, he planted the seed of determination inside Cal, the need to be somebody, the drive to be great, to make this world sit up and take notice of him.

If his mom was alive she'd say, "It only matters what God notices, and He will still notice even if you don't win."

Maybe when your mom said God made you great, she wasn't talking about your pitching.

But Cal, like his father, was not a great man, and he knew it all too well. He was selfish and arrogant and he filtered everything through the lens of his own athletic success. At the end of the day, who cared about Cal Crawford now that his mom was gone? Uncle Oscar and Sweets. A few friends who would drift away if his pitching contract ended.

Gina.

But maybe he had severed that tie with his cruelty and arrogance.

He shook his head to rid himself of the thoughts, but they would not go.

"God," he said, standing suddenly. It was as far as he got. The quiet empty clubhouse mocked him. He did not know what to say to God. He had only questions. *Why did Dad leave? Why did You take Mom? Why am I sitting in this office at five a.m. with a multimillion dollar contract and the feeling that I have nothing?*

Knock it off, he told himself. *You have a job to do and these ridiculous thoughts are getting in the way.* Savagely, he jammed the note into his pocket unopened and strode off.

FIFTEEN

Saturday morning sunlight poked through the hotel curtains and awakened Gina. She let Tippy snore a while longer as she dressed for the day, choosing a bright pink shirt to cheer herself, paired with a denim skirt. Painstakingly, she'd written down the schedule of events on a hotel notepad and stuck the paper in her pocket. Slathering herself with sunscreen, she mentally prepared for the big day, their next-to-last day in Scottsdale. Pete told her that after the weekend was over, she was free to go.

And she wanted to.

Mostly.

Cal's stinging comments from the night before still throbbed. *I am famous and people are weird about fame, just like I told you before.*

Only she wasn't weird about it because she thought of him as Cal, not superstar Cal. His reaction cut her to the core. It was a sharp correction. He expected people, including Gina, to see him as an elite athlete, and he really did think of her as below his stratosphere.

"Well, not everyone is angling for a way to meet you, you big dope," she muttered, though uncertainty nibbled at the edges of her mind. Might Bill have chosen to help her find a job in order to rub shoulders with the famous Cal? Did he have ulterior motives for bringing Matthew to spring training?

Surely not, but images from the past two days swam before her eyes. All those fans jostling to get a glimpse of Cal, watching his every move on the practice field, the young women who had gone so far as to write 'Crawford' on their bare midriffs and shriek his name when he emerged from the tunnel. How could he possibly see things properly? He was despised when he messed up. And when he was performing well as he had been at spring training? Adored. Worshipped.

She considered what Sweets had said at the ranch. *"He doesn't need worship; that's for God. He needs love."*

Didn't matter what he needed, she was not going to be the one to give it to him, especially after his rude treatment. She brushed her hair and pulled it into a low ponytail. Though she would pray for Cal Crawford, she could not help him with the love part. Not she, the lowly dog sitter and the girl who was not going to lose her heart again so soon, not to him.

"Come on, Tippy. Time for breakfast."

Tippy kept her eyes firmly closed.

"I know you're awake, you big faker. Come on. We've got kids to greet."

With some reluctance, Tippy complied, deigning to eat her breakfast with a sprinkling of Cheeto crumbs. "I'm going to have to write all this down for Mitch," she said, heart squeezing.

Some forty-five minutes later, Gina was installed at a table under a white awning. The grass was bustling with activity. Kids of all ages practiced catching with some of the players. Cal, she noted, was advising a group of wide-eyed teens on pitching technique. The sunlight caught his shoulders, the tanned skin, an occasional shy smile. She thought he looked her way a few times, but she was careful not to meet his gaze.

The younger ones began to toddle over, clutching their parents' hands. Pete had supplied all the materials she'd requested — crayons, tape, white paper, and the Xeroxed outlines. With her scissors and crayons she whipped up a sample and put it on. The floppy paper ears danced around in the wind.

"Who wants to make Tippy ears?" she called to the mingling kids.

A chorus of eager children piped up and she was soon surrounded at the table, helping cut and tape the ears on to the paper headbands, watching the kids color with their chubby crayons. She enjoyed the sense of surety that she always got when she worked with children. It was what she was made to do, what God meant for her to do, and in good time He'd give her an opportunity.

Soon the crayons were rolling everywhere as children applied themselves diligently to the task. Each child was given a chance to don their paper ears and sit next to Tippy for a photo op.

Several dozen children later, Matthew climbed up to the table. Her breath caught in her throat.

"Hey, buddy," she said. "Do you want to make some ears?"

He nodded, still wearing the crumbs from his breakfast toast. She got him started as Bill sat next to him and immediately organized the mess of crayons into a neat row.

"Nice setup you've got here," he said. "I'm

sure it was your idea, a natural teacher."

"Who wouldn't want to make Tippy ears?" she said, though the comment pleased her.

"Vivian said to say hello. She wants to know how to make snowballs."

Snowballs were the little white cookies rolled in powdered sugar that she and Matthew had made for sharing on S day in preschool. "It's an easy recipe. I'll email it to you." Gina could not picture Vivian getting her manicured nails mussed by cookie dough, but who was she to judge? To busy her fingers, she colored and folded another set of Tippy ears.

Matthew finished his ears and hopped off the chair to play with the dog.

"I've been trying to get in touch with you to tell you that there is going to be an opening at Mt. Olive when Mrs. Stein has her bunion surgery." He leaned in. "And I heard at the PTA meeting that she's thinking about not coming back next fall."

Gina's heart beat fast. What she wouldn't give to step into Mrs. Stein's shoes and teach her very own class of first graders. "But . . . why would they want me back?" Her face grew hot. "I mean, after the field trip incident and all."

"I'm the PTA president now," Bill said. "And the new principal and I are golfing buddies. I'm going to put in a good word for you."

"That would be so nice of you, Bill, but . . ."

"What?"

"I mean, this is just a friendship thing, right?"

"What do you mean?"

She rushed on. "There's . . . nothing between us anymore. We both understand that, right? You're happily remarried."

He sat back and smiled. "Of course. Things are going great with Vivian and me."

Relief flooded through her. "I'm happy for you. I just didn't want there to be any misunderstandings."

"Not at all. As a matter of fact, Vivian was the one who suggested I come see you at spring training."

"She did?"

"Yeah. She appreciates how good you were to Matthew when we were split up and how awesome you were when we got back together."

In her relief, Gina almost missed the hesitation. He had more to say.

"And . . . ?" she prompted.

"And Vivian's the chair of the fund-raising committee at Mt. Olive for next year."

Fund-raising. "Uh huh."

"You know Vivian." He quirked a smile. "That woman is competitive. She has put upon herself that it's got to be the best, most successful fund-raising bash in the history of the school. I think it's an ego thing. The presidential inauguration probably took less planning." He laughed, a little nervously, she thought.

"What has she decided to do?"

"An auction." He straightened the already straight crayons. "A big dinner-type event where people bid to meet a celebrity."

"A celebrity." Her fingers felt suddenly cold as she reached for the stapler to connect the ears to the headband she was constructing.

"Yeah. She's got some contacts with some TV personalities and an actor who was on some sitcom or another."

"That's great."

"But you know, what would be really awesome . . ." His eyes shifted to the teen pitching practice area.

Her heart thudded like a jackhammer. Surely, he was not about to say it. The words would certainly not spill out of his mouth.

Bill shifted. "It would be amazing if you could get Crawford to come."

The name struck her like a blow. She

221

stared, stomach sinking. "I don't have that kind of influence with Mr. Crawford. I just take care of his dog."

"Don't give me that," he said, wagging a finger. "I've been following the pictures on Twitter and Facebook. You two are close. He'd do it for you."

"Bill," she said, drilling him with a look, "Did you bring Matthew to spring training to use me to get to Cal?"

"Use you? No. Not at all. We're old friends. I wanted to help you."

"Okay." She swallowed hard. "Just answer me one question then."

He rolled the crayons under his fingertips. "Shoot."

"Would you have put in a good word for me at the school if I wasn't an acquaintance of Mr. Crawford?"

He blinked and his mouth worked. It was a moment of hesitation which spoke louder than a voice shouted over a bullhorn. "Sure."

Incredulity rendered her momentarily speechless. Bill was using her and so was his wife, and worst of all, she'd been blind to it. Cal Crawford had been right about everything.

"So, do you think maybe I could get his email for Vivian?"

Gina got up, jammed the Tippy ears on Bill's head, and left him at the table.

Cal tried calling Uncle Oscar for the fourth time in two days. Finally, he picked up.

"It's Cal, Uncle Oscar. I've been calling and calling. Where have you been?"

"Busy," Oscar said. "How's spring training?"

"Incredible."

"Mechanics?"

"Solid."

"Shoulder?"

"Feels good."

"How's the slider?"

"Getting there."

"Keeping your thumb out of it?"

He'd struggled to keep from snapping the ball with his thumb and middle finger, which put too much stress on the elbow. "Yes, sir. Pressure from the middle and index finger."

"Right."

Cal waited, but his uncle stayed quiet. "Uncle Oscar, is everything okay?"

" 'Course. Did I say otherwise?"

"No, sir, but . . ."

"Right. Everything is okay then."

"May I speak to Sweets?"

"She's busy."

"Busy?"

"Has this phone got an echo?" he snapped.

The muscles in his stomach tensed. "No, sir. Usually she wants to chat and tell me about some nice girl in town she's ready to fix me up with."

"Well, today she's busy. I'm busy, too. Gotta go." His voice dropped a notch. "Glad it's going well, son."

And then he disconnected.

Cal stared at the phone, dead in his hand. A line of kids waited nearby to get their turn with him. He wanted to get into the truck and drive back to the ranch, to put his mind at ease that Uncle Oscar and Sweets were perfectly fine. His mind traveled back to the note from his father tacked to the office bulletin board. It was still sitting unread in his jacket pocket, thrown over a chair in his room.

Why did he have such a feeling of dread?

He looked to the tent where Gina knelt on the floor, next to a kid with paper dog ears on. His feet took him there, without consulting his mind.

"Gina . . ." he started.

Until he realized it was Matthew she sat with. Bill stood there, wearing a cockeyed set of ears, his mouth open, face serious.

They'd been in the middle of a deep conversation, not pleasantries and shooting the breeze, but heart to heart stuff.

Gina did not look at Cal. She kept her attention on Matthew and Tippy.

Bill shot him a smile and sidled over. "Mr. Crawford, it's a pleasure to meet you. I'm a big fan."

Cal took the offered hand and shook. "So you're a friend of Gina's?"

"More than that," Bill said, beaming. "We're like family."

Cal sought Gina's gaze, but still she did not look at them.

Family?

"There's nothing more important than family," Bill enthused. "Say, I was wondering . . ."

"You're right about that," Cal said, offering a friendly nod as he walked away.

Pete caught him before the practice game. "You're up. See how things look for thirty pitches or so."

Cal nodded.

Pete's gaze drifted around the grass as the players disentangled themselves from the fans and headed back to the dugout. "Good idea to bring Tippy, wasn't it?" he said proudly.

"Freddy the Falcon doesn't think so."

Pete laughed. "So. Let's see your best arm today, huh?"

Cal's nerves ticked up. "Something you're trying to tell me?"

"Nah. You were our ace last season . . ."

"Except the last stretch," Cal said, wishing he could erase those disastrous outings from his memory.

"And you're still our ace," Pete said firmly. "So get out there and show us why we write you that big fat check, huh?" Pete's hand gripping his shoulder reminded him that he had someone firmly in his corner, rooting for his success as much as he did.

"Gonna crush it."

"I know you will," Pete said.

Gina and Tippy took their seats for the game. Gina was grateful they'd assigned her a place in the shade. It was a relatively isolated spot with empty seats all around, but they were close enough that she could see the pitcher's mound in every detail. While she waited, she whispered to Tippy.

"Can you believe it, Tip? Cal was right. Bill really was using me." Her spirit sank even lower as she contemplated that it had not only been Bill, but his wife as well. And she'd been so clueless she hadn't even had a suspicion.

Tippy shot out a tongue and licked Gina's chin. Gina knew it was Tippy's way of saying, "You don't need that crummy man and his recommendations. You'll find a job all on your own."

Or it might have merely been Tippy slurping up an errant rainbow sprinkle, left over from her morning doughnut. She so desperately wanted to stand on her own two feet, ever since she was a delicate, spindly child. Through the rounds of therapy, the ruthlessly helpful tutors, the smothering sheltering of her parents, the cheerful physicians. *I can do it,* she'd wanted to scream. *Maybe not the way you envision, but I can do it.*

She would not tell Cal he'd been right. There was no need, since she was going home the next day, and she would likely not see him ever again.

"It's for the best," she told herself, yet it did not cheer her.

The team trotted out of the tunnel, uniforms pristine, and took their places for the National Anthem. Gina held Tippy as they sang. Out of the corner of her eye she saw a camera aimed in her direction.

A man with an oddly perfect mustache and a Falcons cap winked at her.

Wait a minute. She peered closer, gasping. The mustache was perfect because it was fake, and it did not fully disguise Tom Peterson. Clutching Tippy, she scanned for a security guard, but there was none nearby.

Tom shrugged. "Don't worry. I'm not going to hurt you."

"You almost ran me and Tippy over at the beep ball practice."

"I'm sorry about that. Purely a mistake. I'd never hurt either one of you."

She glared at him. "Go away."

"I'm here about the dog," he said, snapping pictures of Tippy as she struggled to be put down to greet the newcomer.

"No, Tippy," Gina said, tightening her hold on the dog. "This is a bad man."

Tom looked stricken. "I'm not a bad man, Gina."

She continued to look for a guard.

"I only want a piece of the pie. I want to be somebody, just for once."

The downcast look on his face awakened a pang of sympathy until she remembered that she had no ability to sniff out ulterior motives. "I want you to leave, Tom. Now."

"I just want to get what's coming to me."

"You'll get it, if Cal gets hold of you."

He gave her a wicked smile and snapped another picture, the flash blinding her. "Tell Cal I said hello. Goodbye, Tippy old scout.

I'll be seeing you soon."

He walked away.

Sixteen

Gina's legs were trembling as she sank back down in her seat. Cal would want to know that Tom was lurking around spring training and she could text him later, but right now he was all about his pitching, completely focused, staring at Julio Aguilera crouched behind the plate. No time to bother him, she told herself.

The smack of the ball in Ag's glove made her flinch. A strike, she gathered from the cheer of the crowd. Cal continued to throw strikes for the three innings he pitched. The beginnings of a perfect game she also gleaned, if they hadn't taken him out to allow some playing time for the other pitchers.

"Kid's got it back," said a bearded fan sitting two rows up from her. "That was the best pitching I've ever seen."

Though the throws looked like nothing more than a blur of white to her, Gina found she was glad, in spite of their recent dustup. If pitching was the only thing he had in his life, she was happy that it was going well for him. She remembered the scowling Cal she'd met the first time at his San Francisco mansion. Now she knew the serious mask he wore was only a cover for someone altogether different, altogether deeper.

He'd forced her to see things with Bill as they were, through her cloud of naiveté, and though he'd been arrogant and cruel about it and the humiliation burned strong, her anger was waning. Even though he was a guy who was adored by millions, Cal Crawford was a lonely man for all his fame, and he had tried to be a friend to her.

She prayed. "God, help him know he's more to You than a pitcher." She thought about the future, when her life was detached from his, how she would see his grave face on the TV like all of his other millions of fans. But she would know that behind the mask was the Cal who played beep ball and supplied doughnuts for her hotel room. Much more than a pitcher.

She swallowed the lump in her throat. She would miss Cal, but their two worlds were never meant to collide, and they wouldn't have were it not for Tippy. She leaned over and planted a kiss on Tippy's knobby head.

"Thanks, Tippy. I sure am going to miss you, sweetie pie."

When the game was over, Cal found her at the clubhouse where she'd gone to let Tippy rest on the shady patio with a bowl of cold water.

"You did a great job today," she said brightly when he came and sat next to her. Tippy scooted over and pawed at his knee.

He found the spot just under Tippy's collar and scratched, melting her into a fuzzy jelly. "Thanks."

"All those strikes. You definitely showed great command today."

He laughed. "You've been listening to the commentators."

"Yeah," she admitted.

He rolled his shoulders. "Feels good, real good. And you did an amazing job too, with all those kids. I think that might be harder than pitching."

She realized from the hesitation in his tone that he'd seen Bill and Matthew with her.

"I want to apologize for the way I spoke to you before," Cal said, after a deep breath. "It was rude and uncalled for."

Her cheeks burned. "It turns out you were right, though. Bill was dangling his son and a job in front of me so he could coerce you into a school celebrity auction."

He sighed. "I'm sorry about that."

"Me too," she said, throat thick. "I should have realized. People really will do anything to get close to celebrities, won't they? Tom Peterson, Bill, all those screaming fans. It's insane."

"Yes, it is. I never wanted that. I've never been comfortable with it. I just wanted to play baseball."

"Well, anyway, it's humiliating that I didn't see it myself, about Bill I mean."

He reached out a hand as if to take hers, then let it fall back to his side. "I'm sorry."

"Me, too."

They were silent, listening to the flapping of the Falcons flag as it flew above the patio.

Cal toyed with his bottle of water. "You know Gina, if it would help you get that job you want, I'll do it."

She started. "Do what?"

"The auction. Make an appearance if I can. Whatever they want me to do."

Tenderness and mortification warred together in her chest. "You would let yourself get auctioned off at an elementary school barbecue?"

He nodded.

"For me?"

"If it would help."

233

She was not sure whether to be insulted that he thought she needed the help or overwhelmed that he'd let himself be trotted out at a school auction for her. Overwhelmed won out. "I appreciate that more than you know, Cal, but I'm going to find my own job, all by myself."

"Atta girl," he said, giving her a gentle sock on the shoulder. Tippy squirmed to be let down.

"Oh no you don't," Cal said, holding her closer. "Not until I'm sure Freddy the Falcon has flown off."

More silence. Then she told him about Tom.

Anger sizzled in his eyes. He slammed his water bottle down in fury, causing Tippy to jerk. "That guy is getting on my last nerve."

"Mine, too."

"I'll inform stadium security and our people. It won't happen again."

"I'm driving back to San Francisco tomorrow anyway," she reminded him.

"Oh yeah," he said, voice flat. "I forgot about that."

"I'll keep Tippy on a short leash, so to speak, until you can make arrangements to have her returned to your dad. Once the media attention dies away and I'm not working for you anymore, Tom won't have any reason to take pictures of us."

Cal did not look placated. "Maybe you should stay here in Scottsdale for another few days. Better security."

"Cal, I have a life. I need to get back to San Francisco and find a job, and your father is waiting for his dog to be returned."

"I guess you're right." Cal took the note out of his jacket pocket. "That's probably what this note says."

"You haven't opened it?"

"No."

"Don't you think you should?"

He stared at her, eyes hard. "Don't care what he has to say. You read it, if you want to. It's probably about Tippy."

She picked up the note.

"Funny how he's so committed to that dog," Cal murmured, staring at Tippy. "Not to his boy or his wife."

Gina opened the note and read it.

Twice.

"Oh, Cal," she said around a clog in her throat.

His eyes met hers. "What?"

Silently she pushed the note to him with fingers gone cold. "You need to read this, right now."

Cal was scheduled to pitch the first three

innings of the game on Tuesday. He did — or at least his mind and body showed up, in spite of the crush of emotions his father's note had awakened. Thanks to muscle memory and the fact that he'd left his heart back at that patio table, he managed to pitch another brilliant performance, near perfect. The buzz in the media rose to a roar. *Cal Crawford, the Ace Is Back.*

The cheers of the crowd and his teammates' affectionate thumps did not seem to penetrate as he walked off the field with Pete.

"Not pitching again for five days," Pete said. "We'll see you back here next week, huh?"

Cal nodded.

"Need a ride to the airport?"

"Gina's dropping me off before she heads back to San Francisco with Tippy. I think she's worried I'll crack up or something."

"Will you?"

"No," he fired back.

Pete gripped his arm. "Before you go, got some good news for you."

"I could use some."

There was a twinkle in Pete's eyes. "Gonna start on Opening Day."

Cal gaped. "I'm the starter?"

"You're our ace, like I said."

"After last season . . ."

"You've got it back, Big Shot. Congratulations."

Pete wrapped him in a bear hug and he clung to his mentor. He'd done it. Redeemed himself to the point where he'd been given the matchless honor of being the starting pitcher on Opening Day. Shocks of pleasure jolted through his nerves.

"So," Pete said, letting him go. "We've got reserved seats for your uncle and aunt and Gina and Tippy. You tell 'em to rest up for opening day, huh?"

Cal's stomach squeezed, pinching off the elation. "Yeah. I'll tell them."

Pete slouched off back to the game. Cal had the odd sense as he stood there that he was being pulled between two worlds. Down the tunnel led back to the ranch, his family, his duty. In the other direction was the ball field, his pleasure, his nemesis, a place to show off his God-given talent. If God had given him both, as he knew his mother would have said, why was he so torn between the two?

Gina stood waiting at the end of the tunnel wearing a backpack, leash in one hand connecting her to a wriggling Tippy who pawed at Cal's shins when he approached.

He dropped to one knee and stroked the

dog. He noticed gray hair on her muzzle and some rigidity in her back legs. "She's stiff. What happened?"

Gina cocked her head. "She's been that way since I've known her. It's arthritis. We're giving her medicine for it. I'm going to write it all down for Mitch."

"Oh. Okay."

As they made their way to Gina's banged-up Volvo, he told her about the honor Pete had bestowed on him.

"That's awesome, Cal. The Falcons' people asked me and Tippy to be there on Opening Day, but I didn't know you would be starting the whole season."

He felt a tingle of pleasure. "Will you come then?"

She shook her head, not meeting his eye. "I'm sure I'll have a job by then. Maybe your aunt and uncle can bring Tippy."

When he didn't respond, she stopped and took his hand. "It means a lot to you, I can tell. I just know your aunt and uncle will be there to cheer you on."

Would they? The message had been concise.

Sweets fell and fractured her ankle. Pneumonia set in. They didn't want to tell you because of training. I'm staying at the ranch to drive Oscar back and forth. I know you won't like it, but there's no one else. Didn't want you to be surprised. Mitch

"She's weak from all the treatments," Cal said.

"I've been praying for her."

She looked at him with those green eyes, the sweet mouth, sincerity and faith twined together in one incredibly lovely face. He pulled her to him, and then he found himself pressing a kiss to her lips. The feeling inside was like nothing else, like his mouth had been born to kiss hers, his arms made to embrace her delicate shoulders and all of his senses coming to life because of Gina. Different feeling from baseball, when the roar of forty thousand fans made the ground vibrate under his feet. This sensation was something gentler, deeper, permeating every cell in his body.

His brain shouted out a cease and desist, but his heart would not obey and held her to him until she pulled back, eyes wide, lips parted.

"Cal . . ."

"I'm sorry," he said, quickly releasing her. "I . . . don't know why I did that. I apologize."

"It's okay," she said quietly. "You've got a lot on your mind and your heart."

They continued their walk to her car, his

239

mind reeling from what he'd just done. Why? How? What had he been thinking? She was leaving, walking out of his life. There was no feasibility or logic in kissing Gina.

He walked on in silence and when Tippy began to tire, he snatched her up. The solid warmth of her comforted him. They'd decided Gina would take Tippy back to San Francisco, and he'd figure out the logistics of handing her over to his father later after Sweets was released. Gina promised to write down all the instructions for Mitch, everything from where to get baby socks to the necessity of keeping car keys out of her reach.

Would Tippy miss Cal and Gina? Did dogs miss people? He remembered Tippy's mournful howl when she'd settled onto his mother's bed.

Oh yes, he thought, *they do.* He hauled in a breath. "Do you think her collar is too tight?"

"No. It's just right."

"Her nails seem long."

"I just trimmed them yesterday."

"Maybe we should wait until after Opening Day to return Tippy to my father."

"Why?"

"She's used to being with you. You need

time to explain it to her and all that."

Gina's mouth quirked.

Explain it? To a dog? Had he really just said that? He was losing his mind.

"Then who will take care of her when I get a teaching job?" Her eyes narrowed. "I am going to get a teaching job, Cal, without Bill's help or anybody else's. I have to be prepared to start at a moment's notice. I could get a long-term sub job at any time."

He nodded, determined not to say anything else that might brand him as a halfwit.

They finally arrived at her car.

She opened the passenger side door. "You'll have to ride with Tippy on your lap. There's no room for your long legs in back unless you stick them out the window."

"I could drive," he suggested hopefully.

"No, you can't," she said calmly. "This is my car and I'm driving. Besides, you need to ride shotgun and keep an eye out for stalkers, right? We'll be at the airport in no time. You'll make your flight, don't worry."

"Right," he said dubiously, folding himself into the front seat while Tippy wriggled to find a comfortable position on his lap. His knees skimmed the dashboard.

Gina's phone rang and she answered. "But I paid the bill," she said after a moment. "No, I most certainly did not rent any movies of that nature. Listen to me . . ."

Five minutes later, she stabbed the phone off. "I have to stop at my hotel. They're implying I've been having wild movie parties and dialing Tibet or something. They're going to charge my credit card."

"It's on my credit card," he said. "I'll eat the charges."

"You most certainly will not, Mr. Crawford. It's the principle of the thing."

He wouldn't mention it, but he found her flared nostrils and the proud tilt to her chin adorable.

She pulled into the hotel parking lot. The temperature had already climbed. "Can you let Tippy sit in the shade while you wait? This will just take a minute."

With some effort, he extracted himself from the car and took Tippy's leash, guiding her to a shady seating area. He tucked the handle of the leash around the leg of a lawn chair. Tippy waggled her behind and set off to commence the sniffing. He pulled out his cell phone to see if there were any messages from Oscar or Sweets. Nothing. He had not told them he was coming and he did not know what to expect when he showed up.

Anger for intruding? Fear in Sweets's face that she would not recover?

Didn't matter what he'd find. He'd missed too many visits with his mom until it was too late. Besides, he thought, teeth grinding, he had to arrange for someone else to care for them — someone besides Mitch Crawford.

Tippy crept along the edge of the grass as Cal stood lost in thought. She snuffled, ears perked. "Don't get too excited, old girl. We're getting back into the car in a minute." Tippy suddenly barked, yanking the leash from under the chair. She raced around the corner of the building where a tangle of shrubs shaded the stucco. He put away his phone and jogged after her.

"Tippy, come here," he grumbled. "It's too hot to chase squirrels."

He heard the jangling of her collar up ahead as he pushed past some purple flowering plants. "Come, Tippy," he tried again. "Well behaved dogs come when they're called, you know."

He listened for the sound of her return and heard nothing. "So much for well behaved." He elbowed past the branches and they caught at his shirt. Emerging into the front parking lot, he blinked, brushing the leaves off his shoulders. "Tippy," he called again. The crazy dog was going to get herself run over by a car. He called louder.

Where had the dorky dog gotten to?

And then his feet caught on something.

Tippy's collar and leash, lying on the cement outside the lobby door.

SEVENTEEN

Gina was pale as milk as they sat in an empty reception room talking to a cop.

"He took her," she said. "Tom Peterson. I know it was him. He called and pretended to be the hotel desk. It was a ploy to snatch Tippy."

Cal looked up from his helpless pacing and nodded. "The guy's been stalking me for years. He's obsessed with Gina and Tippy."

"You have to find her," Gina said to the cop. "She's old. And a picky eater. And she has no common sense whatsoever. She snatches car keys and chews on hairbrushes. She's not street savvy at all."

To his credit, the officer, who had introduced himself as Sergeant Flores, did not crack a smile. "We've got people looking already from PD and animal control and we'll watch the pound, too, just in case she managed to get her collar off by herself and someone turns her in."

"She didn't take off her collar," Gina insisted, near tears. "It's a Bowser Built Special LightWeight Leather Superdog model with a handmade, sturdy buckle. I picked it out myself. I can hardly get it unbuckled and I have fingers. Cal had to help the first time."

"If somebody did take her . . ." Flores said.

"They did," Gina insisted. "You've got to believe me. Please. This is a dog abduction."

Flores's pen paused over his notebook. "What would the motive be? Ransom?"

Cal held up his hands, stomach in knots worse than before his first major league start. "I don't know, but I'll pay to get that dog back. She's . . ." He cleared his throat. "Well, I want her back, that's all. The only person I know who actively despises the dog is Harvey, the Falcons' mascot, but he wouldn't take her."

"We'll check anyway." Flores took a few more notes and gave them his cell number after taking theirs.

"We'll keep you posted," he promised as he left. "We'll do everything we can to bring Tippy home."

Marg, the manager, wrung her hands. "I can't believe this. A dognapping. Please stay here until the situation is resolved. On the house. My bellman is already printing flyers to put up all over town. We all love that dog."

Gina thanked her.

"Should I have a room prepared then?" Marg said.

Gina shrugged helplessly. "I guess so. I can't bear to go back to San Francisco if I don't know . . . until we get her back."

She looked at Cal. He took her hand and they returned to the shady nook where he'd lost Tippy. She held the leash in her shaking fingers.

"It's my fault," he said. "I should have been watching her closer."

"Why did you let go of her leash?" Gina asked.

"Because I . . ." He groaned, guilt crashing over him. "No excuses. I was careless."

She gripped his hand as they walked back to the car. The whole disaster had taken so long he'd missed his flight. He got a message that he was expected to make a statement to the press back at Scottsdale Stadium, so he and Gina dutifully returned.

"Awww man," Pete said, as he walked with them up to the cameras. "Who would snatch Tippy? Man, oh man," he said and Cal heard a catch in his voice. "A nice dog like that."

He gripped Gina around the shoulders.

"Don't you worry now, honey. Cal has a million fans. One of them will spot that dog and we'll get her back. You'll see."

Gina nodded, but Cal saw her lower lip quiver.

They stood in front of a microphone and a sea of reporters with cameras flashing. Gina shrank behind him. He'd forgotten this was not the kind of attention she was used to. In truth he'd never quite gotten used to it either. He read the prepared script that he'd hammered out with the Falcons' PR person and thanked the media and public for their help. Hands immediately shot up.

"Do you think this is an effort to throw you off your game, Mr. Crawford?"

"I have no idea."

"What about you, Ms. Palmer?" a reporter called out. "Do you have any idea why someone might have snatched the dog?"

They had already been told not to mention Tom's name, so Gina settled for a nervous head shake. Camera flashes continued to go off.

"Has there been any contact from the dognappers?"

"No, not at this time," Cal said.

"How will this affect your pitching, Cal?" a reporter in the back said. "Any worries that you'll start to slump again?"

"I don't know what other people are worrying about. I just want my dog back."

"Are you concerned that the dognapper will hurt Tippy?"

The question seemed to hang in the air. He heard Gina suck in a breath.

A man in the back stood up and fired off a question. "Is this retaliation from someone who was angered that you were ready to leave Tippy at the pound not long ago?"

The accusation sent a pain through his gut. Could he have really been thinking straight when he planned to dump Tippy? How had the animal gone from an "it" to a "she" that made him smile even when she was taking off with his car keys or chewing his hoodie to shreds? "That was a mistake," he said finally.

"But . . ." the reporter continued.

"Look. Tippy never did anything to anybody. Whatever mistakes I've made, she doesn't deserve to pay for them. I want my dog back. That's all I've got to say." He looked right at the camera. "Please just give Tippy back," he said.

He took Gina's hand and pulled her through the throng and out the back door. Inside he heard the hubbub of voices, the calm pronouncement of the team manager referring questions or tips to the hotline the police had set up.

He wasn't sure where he was going except that he had to get out of there before he lost control. Gina was sniffling and he did not want to see her break into hysterics on national television, where the clip would find its way into soundbites and Internet sports sites. They didn't stop moving until they got to her car. This time he didn't hesitate, getting behind the wheel, racking the seat back as far as it would go, and taking off at a speed approaching reckless.

He watched her profile, hair flying in the breeze from the open window, her lips twisted in worry, sweet, sincere. He wanted to kiss them again, to take her sadness on him where it belonged.

"What are we going to do, Cal?"

"I'm not sure." He realized he was scouring the bushes as they drove, expecting Tippy to waddle out from underneath the nearest clump of foliage. The sun was mellowing into the horizon, leaving the sky a swirl of sherbet orange. It was getting late. "Let's sort it out in the morning. I'll take you back to your hotel for tonight and then I'm going to do my own search." He felt a rush of irrational fear, as if she too would vanish out his life just as abruptly as Tippy had done. *Don't lose your mind, Cal.*

A mile later, Gina's phone rang. It was Marg.

"I'm so sorry, Ms. Palmer, but we're surrounded. There are reporters camped out in the front parking lot and the back, too. I think they're hoping to get a quote from you or something. I've asked them to leave, but they just move across the street and start filming with their zoom lenses."

"Thanks, Marg." Gina groaned as she hung up. "I just can't face that, Cal. I'm going to start blubbering. I just know it. I'm the world's ugliest crier. My face gets all blotchy and my lips swell. I look like a blowfish."

Hiding a smile, he pulled over to the shoulder of the road, let the engine idle, and took her hand until a thought dawned on him. The perfect solution, albeit a temporary one.

"Let's drive to the ranch. There won't be any reporters there and you can stay until we hear something about Tippy."

Her eyes were wide pools of emerald in the late afternoon sunlight. "Drive all the way? Right now? Don't you want to fly?"

"I'm not going to fly unless you are."

She shuddered, blanching. "I can't."

"Fine. We'll drive."

"I can drive myself. I'll be okay. You can fly if you want to."

"I don't want you driving alone, not when you're upset." He quirked a smile at her. "You're not that good a driver even when you're not upset."

He earned a laugh then and a slow nod. "I'm going to the ranch anyway, so it makes sense."

"Well, okay. I guess that's the best option right now."

He pulled onto the road again and headed for the freeway.

"Cal?" she said in a very small voice.

"Yeah?"

"You don't think anyone would . . . I mean, she's an old dog and a gentle soul. No one could possibly . . ."

He gripped her hand. "We'll get her back, Gina. Don't worry."

As the miles passed they fell into silence, and he found himself praying that his words could be true.

They took turns sleeping and driving. Gina fell asleep after they stopped for gas on the last leg of the trip and didn't wake up again until the car bumped up the steep drive to the ranch in the early Wednesday morning hours. She sat up, dazed, as Cal opened the door for her. Trying to unkink her neck, she got out, his steadying hand on her arm. It took her a moment to remember that Tippy had been snatched. Her heart lurched. Where was she? Had her captor made sure she'd been fed? Been given water? She imagined Tippy left outside chained in the sun. With Arizona temperatures . . .

"Have there been any calls?"

He shook his head. "Not yet." They headed into the kitchen and Cal stopped dead. Mitch sat at the table, eating a bologna sandwich. He did not look surprised to see them.

"Hello. I wasn't sure if you'd come, or when."

Gina's heart squeezed. "Mr. Crawford." She shot a look at Cal, but he was staring moodily with no sign of engaging in conversation. "You need to know. Someone has taken Tippy."

Mitch nodded. "I heard about it on the radio." He pulled at his chin, fingers scrabbling over his stubble in a gesture that she'd seen Cal use. "Hate to think of the poor dog scared or being mistreated. That's why I'm still awake, to be honest. Been bunking in Meg's room on an air mattress. Haven't slept much since I heard. How did it happen?"

"Because I wasn't being careful," Cal snapped. "It was completely my fault."

Mitch didn't say anything.

Cal looked at the clock, which read close to two a.m. "I'm going to go to the hospital first thing tomorrow and see Sweets. Is it okay to borrow your car again?" he said to Gina.

She nodded.

"You can drive over with me," Mitch said. "Doctor's supposed to give us a report in the morning."

"I'll handle it," Cal said.

"No offense, but you haven't been here, son. There's a couple of particulars about her medicines that need clarifying. Not sure you'll know what to ask."

Cal's eyes blazed. "I haven't been here? That's rich coming from a guy who was AWOL for my entire life."

"I wasn't dishing up guilt, just stating facts."

"I don't need you to get me up to speed. I don't need anything from you."

Gina wished she could drag Cal back to the car, to undo the horrible scene unrolling before her. She was not sure if she should stay or leave. It was like watching two cars collide.

Mitch wiped his mouth with a napkin,

pushing the unfinished sandwich aside. "That was a different situation and I'm not making excuses for it. Dealing with the present scenario now. You weren't here and Oscar needed help so I stepped in. It wasn't easy for him to accept assistance, but he did, for Sweets's sake. Maybe you should too."

"I don't have to accept anything from you."

Mitch sighed. "I've been a jerk in my life and I let down a lot of people."

"You got that right."

He stood. "But now I'm doing the right thing. I got a second chance to be a good man and I'm going to do it, even if that makes you uncomfortable. Chances like that don't come along every day."

Cal folded his arms, muscles corded, jaw tight. He stared at a spot somewhere over his father's head.

"Anyway," Mitch said, "I'm leaving for the hospital at eight. I'll see you over there." Mitch walked down the hall and she heard the soft click of the door, the squeal of the air mattress as he lay down.

Cal stood frozen. "This is unreal. Now he's decided to become a good man."

"Or at least do the right thing."

His head snapped in her direction. "Is that

supposed to make it okay, what he did? Am I supposed to forget that he abandoned us, just because he's decided to be noble now?"

"Not forget."

"But?"

"Maybe just allow him to do good now."

"I don't trust him to do good. He's a deadbeat."

She walked over and touched a hand to his chest. "And he can never change?"

Cal remained silent, staring down at her hand. "Why would he?"

"I don't know him, Cal, and I didn't suffer what you did, but I can tell you this, people can change for the better. You are not the same Cal Crawford I met in your mansion that day."

He looked confused. "My pitching is better. I'm back on top."

"That's not what I mean. You have allowed yourself to be great," she said with a smile. "And I'm talking about outside the baseball arena."

"If we're not talking about pitching, I don't follow."

She ticked off the items on her finger. "First, you decided not to leave Tippy at the pound. Second, you've bent over backward to do nice things for me, and third, you were incredible with those kids at beep ball."

His brows crinkled. "That's just small stuff."

"No," she said. "That is the big stuff, the blessings that people will never forget."

"Some doughnuts and pitching to kids?"

"Yes sirree."

"I don't understand some of the stuff you say, Gina, but I sure love to hear you say it." He allowed a small smile and a huge sigh. "Sun will be up soon. You'd better get some sleep." He carried her bag to the small room she had occupied before. "No turn-down service here, and there's probably not much of anything in the fridge."

"That's okay. I packed all the leftover doughnuts. I've got three in my purse." Along with a bag of dog treats. The thought made her heart ache.

He laughed, then shook his head, a sad smile creeping over his face. "Seems like I should see Tippy scooting down the hallway wearing those crazy socks."

Her eyes filled. He went to her then, arms strong and warm around her.

"Thank you for being here," he said, voice muffled in her hair. He nuzzled down until she felt his lips brush against her neck. "You were so good to Tippy."

She froze, pushing him to arm's length. "Don't you talk like that, Cal Crawford."

"Like what?"

"As if Tippy's not coming back."

He blinked. "I don't want that to be true, but . . ."

"But what? Is that what you think?"

"It's just what happens."

"No, it's not."

"It is with me," he said, flinging an arm to take in the ranch. "My dad, my mom, maybe Sweets." He exhaled and the bitter tone dropped away. "They leave me."

Naked grief shone in his expression.

"Listen to me, Cal." She reached up and put her hand on his cheek, turning his head and forcing him to look at her, her mouth close to his. "Tippy is going to come back, and I will never stop being your friend."

He quirked her a doubtful look. "Sure you will. When this is over. If we get Tippy back, she'll return to my father. You're going to go be a teacher and I'll play ball. We will never see each other again, Gina, that's what happens. That's what always happens."

"My Nana taught me that when God gives you a friend, you hang on to them." She stroked his cheek. "I will be your friend as long as you'll let me, even if we're not near each other geographically."

A friend? The word thrummed through her. Looking into those gleaming brown eyes her heart yearned for more from him, but she knew he could not give it. He would not put down his baseball and glove long enough to let love in, and she wouldn't allow another man to distract her from her God-given calling to be a teacher. Famous athlete adored by millions. Dog-loving wannabe teacher who made pierogis on the side. Love couldn't bridge those two different worlds, but friendship could.

"My friends seem to come and go, too," he said, stroking her arm. "I sure couldn't find many when I lost us the championship last year."

"I'm a better friend than that, and besides, all of your baseball glory doesn't mean much to me."

He smoothed her hair with his palms. "No? Because my pitching is fierce at the moment, but you never know about tomorrow."

"What do I care if your screwball goes bad?"

Slowly, a wide smile crept over his face and he laughed in a way that almost filled up the too-silent corners of the old house.

EIGHTEEN

The next morning Gina stumbled into the kitchen to find a note on the table with her name on it. The house was still and she realized Mitch and Cal must have left for the hospital. Her car was gone. Cal had been unwilling to ride with his father.

Heard from Sg. Lopez. They questioned Tom Peterson and searched his home/van. No sign of Tippy. He says he had nothing to do with it. So does Harvey the Falcon. People have been calling the tip line like crazy, but no hits so far. They'll keep looking. Falcons have offered a $5,000 reward. I'll keep you posted.

Her heart sank with each word. No Tippy. Was it the same scenario as it was when people went missing? When each day, each precious hour meant it was less likely the victim would be found unharmed? She swallowed hard and forced herself to go take a shower. The hot water did not chase the worries away. Tippy. Sweets. Cal being in close proximity to his father. Cal would need to go back soon and so would she. What if there was still no word about Tippy?

The ringing of the phone made her turn off the water, wrap herself in a towel, and splash down the hallway as fast as she could go. It was the police. She knew it. Snatching up the phone, she swiped the wet hair out of her face.

A cheerful female voice chattered into the receiver.

Somewhere around the fourth sentence, her brain activated properly. "Did you say hot dogs?" she repeated.

The voice on the other line paused. "Oh, sorry. I thought you were Sweets. I was double checking the barbecue situation for today's practice game at the ranch."

"Practice?" *At the ranch?*

"Oh, wait. I guess Sweets didn't tell you. Can I speak to her?"

Gina explained the situation to Jennifer, who she finally remembered meeting at the beep ball practice. Sweets must have not informed everyone of her illness so Gina did, keeping the details to a minimum.

"I'm so sorry," Jennifer said. "I hadn't heard. We'll cancel, of course. If I call right now I can get everyone on the phone probably. Some of them are coming from quite a ways so I'll have to hurry."

Another defeat. All those little kids amped up about their first "real" practice at the ranch only to have it all cancelled. Sweets and Oscar would move mountains to keep that from happening. But what could she do to change that? Alone and barely able to make toast, without even a car to fetch groceries.

"No," Gina heard herself say. "There's no need to disappoint the kids."

"But how can we do this without Sweets?"

"Don't worry. You just bring plenty of volunteers and we'll provide the food, just like Sweets told you."

"We?"

"Um, yeah. We've got some helpers around here somewhere." If one counted Potato Chip the horse and a grumpy cat. "When did you say you were coming?"

"Noon. But really, maybe it isn't a good idea. Oscar was really excited to set up this practice game, but we can reschedule for another time."

"Not necessary," she said. "Noon it is."

"All right, if you're sure."

"Absolutely. I'm totally positive. Lunch at Six Peaks Ranch, practice game to follow at two o'clock sharp." Gina hung up the phone and checked the time again. Nine o'clock.

262

In exactly three hours a team of hungry eight-year-olds, their parents, and a truck-load of siblings would be coming to the ranch to enjoy a game and the culinary delights of Gina Palmer.

"Okay," she said. "We can do this." Feeling a ripple of determination mixed with terror, she squelched back to her room to find some clothes.

Cal paced the hospital lobby until Oscar arrived with Mitch.

"Son, there was no need for you to come," Oscar said. "Sweets is gonna pitch a fit when she hears you left spring training."

"Let her," Cal said. "You should have told me." He would have added to his lambasting, but Oscar looked tired, old. What scared him the most was the expression of unchecked worry on his unshaven face.

They took the elevator upstairs.

"I'm going to grab us some coffee," Mitch said. "Be back in a minute."

When he left, Oscar smoothed his scruff of hair. "Before you start in, I don't like taking help from Mitch any more than you would, but fact is I can't drive and they won't let me stay the night so I gotta get back and forth. Mitch called me up, dunno how he got wind of it, but there wasn't

263

anybody else who could do it so easily and Sweets said she didn't want the church people waiting on us hand and foot. Only got twenty people in the congregation, and they're busy trying to help the pastor's family 'cuz their baby came three months early."

"I wasn't going to criticize you for letting my dad help."

"You were thinkin' it, I can hear it in your voice. Anyway, don't bust my chops. Feel bad enough I can't drive my own wife where she needs to go. Makes a man feel old. Useless."

Like a pitcher who can't throw. Cal's anger died away. "No busting chops. Tell me about Sweets."

"Dumbest thing," he said. "She fell over a rake in the garden and broke her ankle. While she's been lying here in the hospital, she got the pneumonia."

"How serious?"

"Serious enough," he said.

Mitch returned with cups of coffee, which Cal declined. After a deep breath, Cal followed his uncle into the hospital room.

Sweets was sleeping. Cal was struck by how small she looked, how fragile. The antiseptic smell of the room, the bland beige walls, sent him reeling back to his mother's long battle with breast cancer. The same

264

feelings of helplessness and despair welled up.

Sweets opened her eyes. "Is that Cal?" she said, blinking. "I must be dreaming."

Mitch handed her the eyeglasses on the little table and she put them on.

"Yes, ma'am. It's me."

She shot a poisonous look at Mitch. "Well, I see someone has spilled the beans."

Mitch had the decency to look chagrined.

"You should not have left spring training, Cal Forrest Crawford. That was a reckless and unnecessary thing to do."

"Yes, ma'am."

"Come here, boy, and let me get my hugs since you've been foolish enough to come."

He bent down and put his arms around her spindly shoulders, pressed a kiss on her papery cheek, and fought to keep the worry from his face.

"What's this I hear about Tippy?"

Cal shook his head. "You heard that already?"

"I can't stand that dog, but if she's not returned so help me I will get out of this bed, drive to Scottsdale, and find her myself. Your mother loved her." She sniffed. "And, truth is, I guess I didn't exactly hate her either."

Cal took her hand. "We'll find her. You

concentrate on getting well."

She sighed. "Might be easier for me to take up professional baseball. You guys need a catcher?"

"You're a fighter, Sweets. You're going to beat this, just like you beat everything else." He desperately needed to hear the certainty in her voice, the spirit.

"I'm not sure this time, Cal," she said, crushing his heart a little bit more.

He grabbed her hand. "God, please take care of Sweets." At first he hadn't realized he'd said the words out loud, until a look of wonder washed over her face.

"My sweet boy," she said in a whisper. "That is the best medicine I could ever be given."

Tears sparkled in her eyes and he went alternately cold then hot. Had he really prayed? Had God heard? He wasn't sure. All he could do was stand there dumbly and hold onto his aunt's hand as if he were an eight-year-old child again.

The doctor came in to conduct the exam and the three men stepped into the hallway. When the report came, it was not encouraging.

"She's weakened from all the chemo treatments and we're having trouble getting a handle on the infection," the doctor said.

"We've started a new, more powerful antibiotic, but it's our last option."

"Could she get better care at another hospital? A private facility?" Cal blurted.

The doctor arched an eyebrow. "She's getting stellar care here, Mr. Crawford. We're one of the top medical facilities in Northern California, believe it or not."

"I'm sure she is," he said, realizing he'd offended. "I apologize. I'm just worried about her. I want to help in some way."

"The next few days will be critical, and when she does go home . . ." he eyed Uncle Oscar. "She will need care. A nursing home, perhaps."

"No," Oscar growled. "No nursing home. No way."

"I understand you live in a very small trailer," the doctor said to Oscar. "That's going to be hard for your wife to get around. She'll be using a walker for a while and you've got some front steps, I understand."

"I'll put in a ramp. It will be okay."

"At the minimum, she'll need nursing care, physical therapy at the hospital, so there will be plenty of driving back and forth required. Can you provide that?"

Oscar's mouth worked, stark helplessness in his grimace. "I'll do it. Somehow."

Inwardly Cal groaned. He would not want

to insult his uncle for the world, but how could he make sure Sweets got the care she needed? They thanked the doctor and he left. The three of them stood in silence.

"Uncle Oscar," Cal said. "You've got to let me help."

"No nursing home," he snapped. "Just like I said. I'm going to take care of her."

"All right. Then you both come and live at the ranch for a while until she's better. I will hire in-home nursing care."

"I don't need your money and I won't take charity."

Cal ground his teeth. "It's not charity. You are my family. You taught me to play baseball. You and Sweets are the reason I got my shot in the majors."

"You're my son. That's why we care for you," Oscar huffed. "Sorry, Mitch, but I always thought of him that way."

"You were more of a father than I ever was," Mitch said.

"A father doesn't expect to be paid back for loving his kid. It's not like a transaction."

"I know." Cal prayed, in that moment, for a small measure of his mother's empathy and tact. "Please come stay at the ranch and let me hire a nurse, not because I owe you, but . . ." he gulped. "Because I love you."

Oscar's cheeks reddened. "I appreciate that son, but what's next? You gonna retrofit the ranch? Hire me a driver?"

"If you need it."

"Don't need outsiders doing my job. I'm her husband and I'm gonna take care of her. Not outsiders, hear me, Cal?"

"Then I'll do it."

"You can't. You gotta contract."

"I'll break it. I'll walk away."

He stabbed a finger in Cal's direction. "You sure as shooting won't. Your aunt would never speak to either one of us again, not to mention what your mother will say to me when I pass on up to meet her."

"I can't go and play baseball and leave you and Sweets to fend for yourselves."

"We been fending for ourselves just fine."

"That was before the pneumonia and a broken ankle."

His face went dark. "We'll manage."

"Uncle Oscar . . ."

Mitch cleared his throat. "I don't know if it's right for me to offer, but I can be the driver and stay at the ranch until she's better. I can rig up a ramp at the ranch, too. I helped my neighbor do that a couple years ago."

Cal's stomach clenched. "No . . ." he

started, and then he remembered what Gina said.

Not forgetting. Just allowing him to do good.

He took a deep breath. "Uncle Oscar, is it okay with you?"

"If we're gonna get booted out of our home and have some nurse caring for Sweets, at least it'd be good to have Mitch do the driving."

Cal looked at his father. "Doesn't that disrupt your life?"

He shrugged. "It's just me and Tippy . . . Well, it's just me. Got a little place about an hour from here. I'll ask the neighbor to grab the mail. Not much but bills anyway."

"I don't want to ask you to do this," Cal said.

"You didn't ask."

It still grated on him. Mitch Crawford, stepping back into their lives like some sort of a hero, doing what Cal should be doing for his aunt and uncle.

Allow him to do good.

He stayed quiet for a long moment. "All right."

Mitch nodded. "I'll go drive over to my place and arrange a few things."

He looked taller as he left, his tread a little lighter. Though his own gut still twisted with resentment and worry, Cal found his own steps did too, as he walked slowly with Uncle Oscar back toward Sweets's room.

"There's nothing fun about this," Oscar grumbled.

Cal fell in stride next to him. "Yes, sir."

"Never did imagine I'd be leaning on Mitch Crawford for help."

"Me neither."

"Figure God's shoring up our characters with all this business?"

"I don't know how much more shoring up I can take," Cal said.

"You and me both." He clasped his uncle in another bone-crushing embrace, overwhelmed at how much he loved this man and the woman lying in that hospital bed. All the fame, all the celebrity, could not come close.

A scream from the hospital room made the hair on Cal's neck stand up. He took Oscar's arm and they hurried inside.

"What is it?" Oscar demanded. "What's wrong?"

Sweets clasped one hand to her puff of hair. "Hot dogs!" she moaned.

NINETEEN

Gina found the number for a taxi cab, which seemed to be the only taxi cab company anywhere near Six Peaks. It took some forty-five minutes for Gabe, the driver, to arrive with his radio blaring, and another thirty zydeco-filled minutes to get her to the only small grocery shop in town.

"Hot dogs," she panted as she raced into the store. "I need bushels of hot dogs."

The older man behind the cash register snapped into action, introducing himself as Doug, the store manager. "Hey, aren't you Tippy's gal?"

"Yes," she said, filling her basket with ten packages of hot dogs.

"Any word on that little critter?"

"No."

"Now, don't you get discouraged. I'll bet someone's taking real good care of her."

"I hope so."

"Cal gonna be able to pitch with that dog

on his mind?"

The dog was only one of the heavy items weighing on Cal Crawford's mind, she thought with a pang. It made her more determined than ever to pull off the hot dog luncheon for the beep ball kids.

"Hey, now," Doug said with a frown. "I just remembered something. Charlie's bread truck broke down this morning. We didn't get our bread today."

"I don't need bread. We're having a hot dog barbecue."

"But Charlie's the bun guy, too."

She stared. "No buns, Doug?"

"Not a one, Miss Gina."

"How are we going to have hot dogs without buns?"

"Gee, I sure am sorry about that."

"Never mind. You round up the condiments and I'll think of something."

In ten minutes she was out the door again. Gabe helped her pack the groceries into the trunk, and they listened to another round of zydeco music on the way back. She considered trying to boil the hot dogs, like she'd done for her nieces when she'd taken care of them last summer, but eighty dogs was going to be more than she could manage in the one small pot she'd seen in the kitchen. It would take several batches.

The grill. She spotted it as soon as Gabe deposited her at the ranch. It was a massive thing, blackened and dust-covered, but she'd seen a bag of charcoal in the kitchen closet. Quickly she washed the soot-covered grates. It was already after ten. She did an Internet search, landing on some articles entitled, "You and Your Barbecue," and laid out the coals like it showed in the embedded YouTube video. Fortunately, the charcoal was supposed to be "self-lighting." She found some matches, set it to the charcoal, and waited while the coals achieved the stipulated gray, ashy appearance.

Throwing a tablecloth over the old picnic table, she put out the condiments and chips, paper plates and cups. At eleven, she was mixing up a batch of instant lemonade, dumping in all the ice she could find from the freezer, and heaving it out to the picnic table before dashing back inside to the stove. Almost twelve. She decided to do a test batch on the barbecue. A package of hot dogs went down perpendicular to the slats so as to achieve the "mouth-watering grill marks." Smoke billowed, bathing her face in sweat. She figured she would likely never get the smell out of her hair.

At the stroke of noon three cars pulled up almost simultaneously. Kids piled out along with their parents. The little blond boy she remembered walked up, holding his father's hand.

"Hey, Mark," she said. "It's Gina. I'm happy to see you again."

"Hiya." He listened for a moment. "Where's Tippy?"

His father must have heard the news. Bending down, he patted the boy's shoulder. "Remember how I told you Tippy got lost?" He looked at her. "He heard the reporter talking on TV. I told him Tippy wandered off."

"But the TV guy said she got snatched. Like a bad person took her. Did you get her back yet?"

Gina swallowed. "Um, no. Not yet. But I know she'll come back soon, Mark."

"I've got the bases in my car," Mark's dad said. "Let's get 'em set up so we can have the game right after lunch, okay?"

Mark nodded and followed his dad to the car.

Rachel was next, with her mom and dad, followed by three more kids. Without fail, every single one asked about Tippy when Gina said hello. Her heart sank a little bit lower every time she had to tell the kids that Tippy had not been found. She braced herself as the next car arrived — only this one looked familiar. It was her own, and Cal got out, Mitch pulling up behind in his vehicle.

Cal took in the scene. "How in the world did you manage this?"

"Well . . . I . . ." She felt puffed up with pride until his eyes rounded. The smell of burning meat wafted to her nostrils.

The hot dogs!

It was too late. Cal raced for the barbecue, which was now shooting up billows of yellow flames. He grabbed the tongs, yanked off the blackened cylinders, and shut the lid to smother the fire.

The hot dogs smoldered in the dirt, shrunken and black.

"Oh man. I forgot about them." She stared at the smoking mess. "I wonder if they got any good grill marks before they went up in flames."

He smiled. "I think I saw some grill marks on there. They're just hard to see through the burned stuff."

She kissed his cheek. "That was sweet. How is your aunt?"

Cal took in the milling parents and kids. "Hanging in there. She suddenly remembered she'd committed to the beep ball barbecue and told us if we didn't get over here pronto she would call the police and have us tossed out of the hospital."

"I had it all handled," Gina said, "except for the flaming dogs."

"No problem. You did a great job." She could see the smudges of fatigue on his face. She clasped him around the arm. "I wish Tippy was here to go visit Sweets. Deep down, she loves that dog."

He smiled, but it did not reach his eyes. "Bringing her to the ranch. My dad is going to stay here."

He could hardly choke out the word *dad*.

"That was hard to accept, huh?"

"Like swallowing glass."

"How can I help you, Cal?"

He offered another exhausted smile. "You've already helped way more than we could have asked."

She did not like the defeat in his tone. "Well, now that you're here," she said, pulling the kitchen towel from her back pocket and tucking it into his, "you're the new grill master."

She brought out the rest of the hot dog supply while Mitch began to help the kids pour lemonade into paper cups. Cal grilled up the hot dogs, handing platters of them to Gina. Avoiding Cal's gaze, with as much dignity as she could muster, she plopped each hot dog on top of a pancake and handed them out to the puzzled children and parents.

"There was a small situation with the bread supply," she announced. "So we're serving hot dogs in blankets. Who wants one?"

All the children squealed with glee.

Cal stood, tongs suspended in midair. "Only you could come up with that idea, Gina."

"You're right, Mr. Crawford. I am nothing if not a creative problem solver."

He sighed. "Could have used you at the hospital. I've got plenty of problems that need solving."

While the kids munched their dogs in blankets, he told her more details about Sweets coming to live at the ranch and Mitch's offer to drive.

She reached out to him. "That sounds like the best solution."

"But I should be taking care of her, not Mitch."

"You are taking care of her, by helping her move in here with Oscar and arranging a nurse and . . ." She squeezed his shoulder, hardly making a dent against the rock hard muscles of his pitching arm. "And by allowing Mitch to come. That's taking care of your aunt, Cal."

"I guess," he said. "So, um, can you stay for a while longer? Keep me company here for a few days until I go back to spring training? Sweets would love it."

"And I would too, but I can't."

"Why not?"

"I got a job offer."

He stared. "Yeah? Where?"

"It's not what I was hoping for. It's a long-term sub job in Florida."

"Florida?"

She nodded. "I grew up there. I emailed one of my high school teachers and she asked for me when she goes out on maternity leave."

"But that's high school. You want to work with little kids, don't you?"

"It's like the minors, Cal. You have to put in the time and prove yourself."

"Florida, though. I thought you would stay in California."

"This coming from the guy who travels seven months of the year. Your home is where the mound is, right? I guess my home is where the classroom is. I can stay with my parents for a while. They'll love it."

He looked into her face with eyes so grave she felt as if she had betrayed him somehow. She trailed a finger along his forearm. "We'll still be friends, Cal, no matter where I am

279

or where you are."

"When do you leave?"

"At the end of the month. I'll help Mrs. Filipski as much as I can, then I'll hop a Greyhound and get going."

"But what about when they find Tippy? We're starting the season soon."

"She's going back to your father, Cal, remember? You don't need a dog sitter anymore."

"Yeah," he said, pulling away. "I guess I don't."

"But I'll text and phone and come to see you whenever I can," she said, trying to put the smile back on his face and ease the pain that had suddenly formed in her heart.

"Yeah, sure," he said. "Looks like it's time to play some ball."

Cal thought long and hard, staring at the dimming light reflected on the surface of the pond. It was after sunset and the kids had played to their hearts' content, gobbled up the hot dogs in blankets, and taken turns petting Potato Chip. It was good to hear the squeal of kids on the ranch, infusing the place with an energy that had been long absent. Mitch had left the beep ball activities midday and gone to the hardware store, returning with boards to begin construction on the ramp for Sweets.

The splashes indicated the fish were searching for their fill of mosquitos, including the one fish Gina had tossed back in after her triumph over the slippery monster. Her fishing skills were just one in the long line of Gina surprises. The biggest surprise of all was the way he could not get her out of his mind. It made no sense.

His pitching was the best it had been in his whole career. He was starting in the season opener. Sweets would recover and he'd keep the ranch, at least for a while. So why, then, did it feel like he'd taken a fastball to the gut?

It was the worry about Tippy, he told himself. But Gina and Tippy were inexplicably mixed in his heart for some reason, and he was losing her too, in spite of her reassurances. She'd move on to a new life, new friends. He tossed a branch into the pond. A new love.

If only she'd stay close, find a job that she loved. She could stay in California and they'd be connected when he was home in the offseason. And Tippy would be back, he felt it. She'd be returned and Gina would come to visit. He remembered her there on his ridiculous front lawn in San Francisco, hair flying, cheeks pink with joy, tossing the ball to Tippy, who would probably never in this lifetime learn to fetch it. The smile drifted across his face. If she could stay . . . if he could only keep her from leaving.

The idea jolted him as he hiked back to the guesthouse. It took only a few minutes of Internet research to find the contact info. A few more minutes and the task was done. Gina would have the job she loved, she'd stay in California, and he'd be able to see her during the offseason. Triple play.

Finally, he was able to stretch out on the bed and sleep.

TWENTY

Cal rose before sunup and ran for a couple of miles along the trail that paralleled the river. He planned to go visit Sweets and return to help Mitch get the ramp in place, contact some homecare nurses recommended by the hospital, and try to hire one that could both stand up to Sweets and deal with Oscar.

Gina was in the kitchen, holding a cup of coffee, frowning at her phone. "I was checking for news of Tippy. Nothing." She sighed. "Then I got this weird message from Mt. Olive School. It sounds like they want to make me a job offer."

He poured coffee for himself, hiding his smile. "That's great."

"It's so strange, though. I told Bill in no uncertain terms that I didn't appreciate being used by him to get to you and he should find another celebrity for his auction."

"I don't mind doing the auction thing.

It'll be fun."

"But . . ." she broke off, eyes round. "Wait a minute. Did you do this?"

"Do what?"

"Did you call Mt. Olive and tell them you'd do the auction if they'd hire me?"

"Not exactly."

"What did you do?" Each word fell like a cutting fastball. "Tell me, Cal Crawford, right now."

He began to get an inkling in his gut that this wasn't going the way he'd anticipated. "I knew you wanted to work there. I called the principal and told him what an amazing woman you are and sent him clips of you helping the kids at spring training."

Her face went rosy. "You didn't."

"I did, and I told him I'd be happy to do the auction thing too, but that was just a side note."

She pressed her lips together in a tight line. "I cannot believe you did that."

"But it's good, right? It's what you wanted? To work at Mt. Olive?"

"I wanted," she said, sounding like she was speaking through clenched teeth, "to get a job on my own merits, rather than having it bought for me."

"I didn't buy it for you."

"Yes, you did. You used your fame to get

me a position." Angry tears sparkled in her eyes. "That's humiliating. Why did you do it, Cal?"

"I thought I was doing something nice for you."

"Was it for me? Was it really for me, that you did this?"

He held up his palms. "What do you mean? Of course it's for you."

"I mean," she said, voice breaking, "you were doing something nice for you."

He fisted his hands on his hips. "How was this for me, exactly? I don't want to teach there."

"Be honest, let go of the macho thing for a minute. You wanted me to stay close, to you, to the ranch, to be here when you come back to visit, didn't you? That's the real reason you arranged all this."

He could not deny it.

"You were being selfish, just as selfish as Bill was. He used Matthew to get to me, and you're using my job. Well, you know what? Friends don't do that."

"I . . ."

"Friends believe in each other and support each other, and they stay together because they want to, not because it's engineered. A real friend would believe that I could do it by myself, Cal." She sat

285

ramrod straight in the chair.

"Gina . . ." he said as she shoved her chair back from the table and stood. "I was trying to help out a friend."

Her anger changed to puzzlement. "Is that really what we are? Friends? Or is there something more than that?"

He felt paralyzed. What should he say? How could he answer? The way she looked at him, the kiss . . .

"Cal," she said. "Tell me the truth. Did you arrange all of this just to keep a friend around?"

Did he? Was he so desperate to have her stay close because he treasured her friendship? Strange shocks of emotion jolted through him as he remembered the feeling of her body in his embrace. "That's it," he heard himself say. "Just friends."

The green eyes shimmered and dulled, the light of anger fading away and taking with it something else.

"Like I said, I'll always be your friend, Cal," she said, "but I'm still going to Florida. I hope everything works out the way you want it to here at the ranch, I really do." She got up from the table and went down the hallway to her room, hugging herself around the waist and looking very small.

What had he done?

Tried to help a friend? It didn't ring true in his own heart. He should go after her, explain, find the courage to tell the truth, whatever that was, but his feet remained frozen in place. It felt like his disastrous showing last season when he'd tried so hard, done everything he'd been told, and still the ball would not obey his command. Out of control. He could only fester in that horrible feeling, as he heard her toss her things around, packing up.

Later, he carried her bag to the car, accepted the stiff hug she offered, and stood staring as she drove away.

Game over.

He'd never felt so alone in his entire life.

Gina had to pull off to the shoulder several times when the tears made driving unsafe. Cal had done a bonehead thing, disregarding her feelings and pride, and for that she could forgive him. But what hurt was that he'd let her drive away with the realization that he did not love her, not enough.

Love. She had not even admitted to herself that her feelings for Cal had transcended friendship. When had it happened, exactly? When he'd brought her to the ranch and she'd seen clearly the type of man he was?

Honorable, wounded, loyal to his family and to her? When he'd driven across half of Arizona, searching every corner and bush for Tippy, the zany dog who'd turned his life upside down? She could not pinpoint when her feelings had morphed from friendship to love, but it hardly mattered now.

Friend or something more, she was a commodity to be kept around, a girl who could be contracted to stay in his life, neatly arranged for like the tidy furnishings of his San Francisco home or the staff of people who provided for his care and comfort. How mortifying. Her cheeks went hot again.

She was not being fair, she realized. She was more than staff to Cal, but it was a lopsided relationship. On her side, love. On his? Something else.

"Big fat deal, Gina. You loved before, you'll love again. Take care of yourself and get packing." Her insides ached anyway, and the miles passed in agonizing slow motion without Tippy to keep her company in the passenger seat.

When she finally arrived back in San Francisco, she let herself into her tiny room. There was a text message on her phone from Cal.

Let me know when you arrive.

Home, she texted back. It was not true.

She was not home, merely in a borrowed bed in a room that seemed so far away from the joy and laughter she'd been blessed to enjoy since the day she'd met Tippy and Cal. Where was home? Greeting cards said it was where the heart was. And her heart lingered at a rundown ranch with Cal, and somewhere lost in the night with a sweet old dog who couldn't help but love everyone.

Once again she folded her hands and prayed for Tippy to come home . . . and for Cal.

Cal wrenched up a few nails from the corner of the ramp that did not meet his standard of perfection. The weeks had passed in a torturous rhythm, unless he was pitching. He'd returned to spring training, shuttling back and forth to the ranch whenever he was off, until training was over and he went home for the final time before the season opener.

He was not supposed to be hammering nails, but he did anyway. It did not seem important at the moment to protect the million-dollar hands. There was work to be done and he would soon have to catch a plane for their first game. Besides, busy was best. Busy prevented his heart and mind from running amuck with thoughts about how he'd messed things up with Gina and the persistent silence about Tippy. When his phone rang, he snatched it quickly, shaking the sawdust from his hair.

"Don't hang up."

"Who is this?"

"Tom Peterson."

Cal was about to push the disconnect button when he heard one word.

". . . Tippy."

Rage boiled through him. "You took her, didn't you?" He clutched the phone. "I'm going to find out what you did to her if it's the last thing I do, and you're going to pay for it."

"Listen to me," Tom said, nearly yelling. "I didn't take her, but I finally know who did."

"And I'm supposed to believe that?"

"It's the truth. Why would I be calling you otherwise?"

"Why?" Cal tried to keep from shouting. "Because you're nuts and all you want is your five minutes of fame and you've been stalking me and Gina, invading our privacy, all to get your name in the paper."

"Okay. I've done some bad things, but I didn't touch Tippy. I wouldn't hurt her."

"You almost ran her and Gina over."

"That was an accident. I like dogs and Gina's a nice lady."

"I'm going to hang up now and call the police again, and you can tell them your latest story."

"I can get Tippy for you."

Cal stopped. "Why should I believe you?"

"Because you want your dog back."

The truth of that sprang alive in his gut. He wanted Tippy returned, that crazy dog who had twined her crooked way around his heart. He loved the old animal, and her loss left a hole in his heart right next to another one.

But Tom was no doubt manipulating him again, using him to get what he wanted. Guilt pounded in him. Hadn't he done the same thing with Gina? Arranged for her job just to keep her close without the messy prospect of revealing the jumble in his heart?

What do you want, Cal? his mind hollered at him. *What did God put you down here to do? Pitch? Run? Love?* His brain whirled. "What do you want, Tom?"

"If I get Tippy back for you, I get to be the hero."

"You're not a hero," he spat. "You're a stalker."

"For one minute, just one time," he pleaded, "I get to be the guy, the one who

291

gets some attention for being great. That's not too much to ask."

He thought of Gina then.

You've changed.

Maybe just allow him to do good now.

He looked across the yard at Mitch who knelt on hands and knees, checking the boards with a level. Never in a lifetime would he have imagined himself to be working on a project with his father. Was Cal Crawford the kind of guy who could allow someone else to be great?

"Cal?" Tom said. "Are you still there?"

"Yeah, I'm here."

"Have we got a deal?"

Cal considered for one moment more. It was time to be the kind of man Gina and Tippy believed him to be. "All right. Rescue my dog and I'll make sure the whole world knows it."

"I'll be in touch," Tom said as he clicked off.

He checked on the nurse, stocked the refrigerator, and swept the already clean kitchen. He'd just settled onto the sofa with a bottle of water when his father came in, face sheepish.

"Hey, uh, sorry to ask, but could you give me a ride to my place? I locked my keys in the car and I've got a spare set back home."

Inwardly, Cal groaned. The last thing he wanted to do was spend forty-five minutes sitting next to his dad. He'd been using Sweets's pickup since Gina had left in her Volvo, and there didn't seem to be a way to decline the request.

"All right."

They climbed into the truck and Cal headed into town and on through, taking the main road out to the even smaller town where his father had bought a house.

"What made you pick this place?" he said as the truck bounced along the gravel road, sending rocks pinging underneath.

"Cheap, and close to Meg."

Could have been close to her when she was well, he thought, but he bit back the remark. There were only a few houses along the road, spaced far apart. His father's house was small, no more than one bedroom, he imagined, sitting on a rock-strewn lot with a row of pine trees that sent a cascade of needles onto the worn shingles.

"It might take me a minute to find the keys," he said. "Come on in."

"No," Cal wanted to say, but his father was already out of the truck and opening the front door. With a sigh, Cal followed.

He skirted a warped board on the porch and entered the tiny house. It was a mess, a sagging sofa stacked with boxes, a crate which served as a coffee table covered with camera parts. In the kitchen there were cereal boxes and empty frozen dinner containers. As his father went back into the bedroom, Cal examined the camera flotsam strewn around. They were old cameras, the kind with levers and dials that required actual film and developing to do their work.

He remembered his father taking one apart, reverently showing a little boy Cal all the insides. Cal had not cared at all, thinking only about escaping outside to fish or play ball.

All these cameras, old, discarded, obsolete. There was something sad about it and the way his father still cared for these useless things. Cal wished he'd cared more when he was younger, or at least pretended to.

He crossed to a set of shelving. There was a photo there, dusty, of Cal and his dad standing together, smiling. It had been taken at the pond. Cal was holding a good-sized fish, grinning madly.

"I never was a good fisherman," Mitch said. "Your mom helped you catch that one, but she insisted that I be in the picture with you." He stared at the photo. "She was like that, always seeing me as a better father than I really was. She had an optimistic life lens, she told me once."

He felt a pain in his heart. "Yeah." She'd seen the best in her son, too.

He noticed that the photo was propped next to a Bible with a worn purple cover. His mother's. It was free of dust, as if it had been recently moved.

"She gave it to me before she died," Mitch said. "She was hoping I'd learn to pray. That optimistic life lens thing again."

"Did you?" Cal wondered why he'd asked the question of this man he despised.

"Not yet. She said she was going to pray double headers until I could manage it myself." He laughed. "She was constantly writing notes and calling me up to tell me how she'd prayed for me."

A woman with so much disappointment and struggle in her own life who always found the time to pray for others. An ache balled up inside him, and at that moment he thought he'd drown in the sorrow.

Mitch took the Bible and fingered the cover. "I told her I was a slow learner so she said to write it down, what I'd pray for, if I could." He took a piece of paper out of the Bible. "I wrote it, just like she said."

"What did you write, Dad?" He was not sure why he wanted to know, but something way down deep in his soul craved the answer.

His eyes wandered over the pieces of camera and the dust-covered photo magazines. "Your mom said that God is a Father who forgives every bonehead thing we've ever done and He loves us anyway, all the time, and never lets us down, ever."

Cal heard the throb of regret in his father's voice and the twinge of hopefulness there, too. "Do you believe that?" he asked.

Mitch's brown eyes met Cal's. "I don't know, but I'm going to keep thinking on it and reading some of that Bible and if I learn how to pray someday . . ." He gazed at Cal as if he was lost in the past, looking at his little boy whom Cal realized he'd loved in his own flawed way. He wasn't a good father, a good provider, a faithful man, but he had loved his son in the only way he could.

The muscles of Cal's throat tightened. Inside, the hard crystalline hatred in his heart softened, just a little, just enough.

"Well . . . anyway, this is what I wrote." Mitch unfolded the brittle paper. "I'd pray that my son would know a Father like that, the kind that would never let him down, like I did."

A sizzling mixture of emotion flooded

through him, reaching the places behind the rocked-in spots that had been sealed away since he was a child. *I do know that kind,* Cal realized. *I learned it in the joyful times with Mom and in the heartache of losing you. I do know that God loves me, Cal Crawford, in spite of the messes I make. I feel it, deep down. I know.* He'd been reminded of that long-slumbering truth because of the gentle soul of a young woman and the unconditional love of a dog.

He caught his father's gaze. They would have a long road ahead, a route full of bumps and anger and resentment, but in that moment he had a glimpse of hope that he might know his earthly father because he'd remembered his heavenly one.

"Dad?"

"Yeah?"

"If you're — if everything goes okay, would you come to Opening Day to see me pitch?"

Mitch's mouth fell open. For a moment, he stood stock still, gaping. Then he cleared his throat and straightened a bit, growing an inch before Cal's eyes. "Son, there is no place in the world that I would rather be."

Though he could not decipher all the feelings pinballing around in his heart, Cal knew that something momentous had just taken place. He desperately wanted to tell Gina about it.

His phone buzzed. Blinking, he reached for it.

The shock almost made him drop it.

"What happened?" his father said. "What is it? Is it Sweets?"

He could not answer. Instead, he turned the phone around so his father could see the text.

Mitch gasped. "I sure didn't see that coming."

"Me neither," Cal said, heading for the truck.

TWENTY-ONE

Gina had just put out the last batch of pierogis when Mrs. Filipski screamed.

"Are you okay?" Gina yelled, running into the shop. "Did you burn yourself?"

She pointed to the small TV screen. "Watch. Just watch."

Gina did.

Tom Peterson stood in the glare of cameras, beaming. Tippy wriggled in his arms, stubby legs waving back and forth.

It was Gina's turn to scream. She clapped her hands over her mouth. "Turn up the sound, quick."

The reporter spoke into a handheld microphone. "Thanks to the clever detective work of photographer Tom Peterson, Tippy the dog has been recovered after six long weeks. Tell us how you found her, Mr. Peterson."

"I've been investigating Harvey Bland, the Falcons' mascot. It took me quite a while, but I finally realized he'd taken Tippy to his

299

grandmother's house in Tempe. He told her he was watching Tippy for a friend." Tom laughed. "Harvey didn't appreciate Tippy stealing his thunder."

The reporters buzzed around, peppering Tom with questions.

"What is your relationship with Mr. Crawford?"

"We played a little ball together in college. We're . . . friends."

Friends? Tom Peterson? And Cal?

Gina moved close, scanning as close as she could. Tippy seemed perfectly fine, her normal enthusiastic self. She snaked out a tongue and slurped Tom's chin, eliciting laughter from the group. Gina wished she could reach through the screen and caress the sweet old dog.

Then Cal Crawford walked into the picture, taking Tippy from Tom and shaking his hand. Gina's pulse accelerated.

"I want to personally thank Tom for returning Tippy to me. I can never repay the debt."

"How did you come to be aware of the situation, Mr. Crawford?"

Cal shook his head. "This isn't my story to tell, it's Tom's. He's the hero. I'm just grateful to him for returning Tippy."

Gina realized there were tears streaming

down her cheeks. Cal looked so happy, relaxed, the same handsome face that inhabited her dreams every night since she'd left Six Peaks. *Cal, I miss you, so much.*

"Why are you crying, Gina?" Mrs. Filipski asked. "Happy tears?"

She nodded. She was happy, thrilled, overwhelmed that Tippy had been found safe, thanks to the bewildering actions of Tom Peterson. She was also stricken with grief.

Cal had not called or texted to tell her about Tippy.

"Will this put you in a better mental state for your start on Opening Day next week, Mr. Crawford?"

He waved away the question, tucking Tippy under his arm and heading out of camera range.

Not one word to her, after all they'd been through. Her heart ached.

"Aren't you happy, Gina?" Mrs. Filipski asked.

She nodded. "Yes. Very happy."

"Do you want to go see the dog? We can manage fine without you here."

She shook her head slowly. "No. I've got things to do."

"What things?"

She sucked in a deep breath. "I'm going

301

to print out my train ticket and arrange for a ride to the station on Monday."

"Monday? You're not going to go see Opening Day?" Butch said. "Thought they invited you. You're Tippy's favorite person."

She shook her head. "I'm sure Cal will get someone to be there for Tippy." In spite of the pain rippling through her heart, she knew it was time to move on. Gina was ready for her own opening day, an exciting new season. Now that she knew Tippy was safe, there was nothing to keep her from a fresh start. Cal did not need her or want her.

Pressing the grief down deep, she turned and started up the stairs.

Sunday night, Gina took extra care to paint her nails and wind her hair into pink foam curlers. She vowed to be at her absolute best as she boarded the train for her new life. The blue floral dress and snappy yellow sweater were laid out on the chair next to her packed suitcase. So what if it was chilly? She intended to be as cheerful as she could, at least outwardly, as she took off into her new life.

Early to bed, she figured. She prayed and lay down to let sleep claim her. Stubbornly, it refused to do so. The room was quiet.

Mrs. Filipski was at a movie with Butch and she would not return home to her own room downstairs until late. Gina thought of the conversation she'd had with Sweets on the phone the night before.

"I'm going to be at that Opening Day game if I have to crawl on my hands and knees. Oscar tried telling me no, but you can imagine how that went. Cal's chartered us a plane, booked us limos, a presidential suite, and has a nurse on call, though I told him I won't need it. There's a special seat for me in the ballpark, since I've got to use my wheelchair for now. You come sit with us. I'll tell Oscar to save you a spot if Cal didn't already do it. Mitch will be there, too."

Mitch? Gina breathed a prayer of thanksgiving. God truly was the maker of miracles. She tried again to interject. "I'm not coming to Opening Day, Sweets," she'd said softly. "I'm going to Florida."

Fifteen minutes later she had still not made Sweets understand that she had to say goodbye to Cal and the nutty world of professional baseball and all the crazy trappings that came with it. Stalkers turned heroes, press conferences and reporters around every turn.

"Did Cal tell you he's going to host a beep

ball camp this winter?" Sweets said. "He's going to make a personal commitment to being there for the whole five days, and he bought new jerseys for the Hornets. The kids are over the moon. And Tippy, that hair dropper, is going to live with us at the ranch as long as Mitch does, which will probably be a while since he's been such a help with everything."

Gina felt a thrill of delight, along with a surge of pain. Cal had not told her anything. "That's wonderful."

"Cal says we need to have pancakes with our hot dogs or some such thing, at the beep ball camp."

Her eyes brimmed as she thought about it, how proud he'd been of her attempt to barbecue, in spite of the flaming hot dogs. She'd said she'd pray for Sweets, and maybe visit the ranch in the summer when Cal was on the road.

It was almost nine and she was not feeling at all sleepy. She thought about texting Cal to wish him well for Opening Day, the biggest of his career, she knew, but she thought again of how he had not contacted her when Tippy had been found. The hurt stung afresh. Her feelings were not his. She turned off her phone.

Done feeling sorry for yourself? she chided,

rolling onto her side and trying to find a comfortable position in spite of the curlers. The minutes ticked by with no promise of sleep. A sharp crack made her sit up, heart thumping.

Nothing. Must have been a car backfiring, she thought.

Then a palm hit the outside of her window. She screamed, clutching the blanket with one hand and grabbing her phone with the other. Her fingers shook so much she could not get them to dial 911. A frowning face appeared at the window.

Her scream stopped mid-throat as puzzlement took the place of terror. Cal Crawford was knocking on her window. She rubbed her eyes. He was still there, looking slightly more exasperated now. He mouthed something.

She watched in frozen fascination.

Open the window.

She suddenly came to the conclusion that Cal Crawford really was standing outside her window on the fire escape, gesturing for her to open the window, for crying out loud.

She leaped out of bed, tied on her fuzzy polka dot bathrobe, and wrenched open the window. He climbed inside, holding a backpack.

"What are you doing here?" she finally

managed.

"I tried knocking and you didn't answer your phone, so I climbed the fire escape."

"Why did you come?"

"She won't eat. I think she misses you."

"Who?"

He carefully opened the pack and Tippy popped her head out like a dog in the box.

"Tippy," she squealed. The dog wriggled loose with Cal's help and began to lick Gina on every exposed inch of skin. Gina laughed, caressing and scratching the wriggling coil of canine.

"So Tom really did find her?"

"He did. He was busy stalking me on the practice field and he noticed that Harvey Bland was pretty smug, which made him suspicious, so he decided to stalk him for a while. Took him weeks, but he got the job done."

"You were gracious on the TV," she said. "Tom came across like a hero."

Cal shrugged. "He got Tippy back. He deserves some kudos."

Gina rubbed her cheek against Tippy's silky head. "And you brought her to see me? Now? Sweets said you fly out tonight."

"Yeah." He shrugged. "Actually, I sort of came for me, too."

She became suddenly aware of how gorgeous he was, chocolate eyes gazing at her, slight scruff of beard on his chin, wide, muscled shoulders and the puzzled look on his face as he studied her . . . curlers! Her hand flew to her hair. "Well, I, um, I wasn't expecting a visitor." She began to pull the foam bits from her hair.

"No," he said, stopping her hand. "Leave them. I like it that you're a girl who wears pink foam curlers."

"Why would you like that?"

"Because," he said, fingers tracing the hair wrapped knobs. "You're genuine."

"Genuine, but not very polished." Drat if her cheeks weren't burning again. He was gazing at her in a way that made her stomach do flip-flops.

"You're a woman who eats doughnuts and wears flower prints and puts socks on Tippy and serves hot dogs in pancakes. I never met anyone like that before."

"Probably not." She put a wriggling Tippy on her bed. The dog immediately burrowed under the blankets and found the warm hollow Gina had just vacated. "But Cal, did you hit your head? You're not making sense, coming here chatting about doughnuts and curlers."

He started to pace in little circles. "Listen," he said. "I gotta talk right now."

307

She looked for the signs, dilated pupils, a bump on the head. "Do you need to sit down?" She shot a glimpse at the clock, breath catching in horror. "Cal! It's nine fifteen."

"I know."

"Sweets said your flight was at ten thirty."

"It is."

"But if you don't make your flight tonight they won't let you start. Aren't those the rules?"

"Yeah."

"You've only got an hour to get to the airport."

"I know."

"Then what are you doing here?" she yelled, grabbing him by the arm and eliciting a bark from Tippy who periscoped her head out of her burrow. "You've got to get to the airport right now."

"I need to be here more." He bent to pat Tippy. "You know the best thing about this dog?"

She could only gape.

"She loves me, even though I tried to take her to the pound. I was ready to throw her away and she still loves me just as much as before. I mean that's some kind of forgiveness, isn't it?"

"Cal," Gina said very slowly and calmly.

308

"You are having some sort of mental collapse. Go sit in the car, and as soon as I get dressed, I will drive you to the airport where your team doctor can check you over." She was going for her shoes when he stopped her by taking her hand.

He shook his head. "I'm here to tell you the truth. I did arrange that Mt. Olive job for selfish reasons. I wanted to keep you around." He cleared his throat. "Because I love you."

She blinked, frozen. "What?"

"I love you."

She had heard correctly. He'd said he loved her. She could only stare in dumb astonishment.

"I tried to pretend you were just a friend, but that's not the truth of it. I love you."

Her lips tried several times before the words came out. "What . . . well . . . why would you do something like that?" she stammered.

"What?"

"Fall in love with me? I'm not of your world."

"Yes, you are. My world is my family. Baseball is my job. Took me a while to get that straight."

Her pulse began to hammer. "Cal, you came here tonight to tell me this knowing that you would miss your flight?"

He didn't answer.

"You are turning your back on the biggest game of your life, for me?"

Something in the way he cocked his head, drank her in with his brown eyes, made her quiver inside.

"You are my life. Nothing else matters if you aren't in it. Not the pitching, not the fame, nothing."

Tears pricked her eyes and she caught her lip between her teeth. This couldn't be happening, couldn't be real, but he was still staring at her, hands caressing her shoulders.

"I have so many people telling me who I am and what I should be, but you see me the way God made me."

"He made you great, Cal Crawford," she whispered.

"And you make me want to be a great man, not just a great pitcher."

Tears wobbled on her lashes. "I'm so happy, Cal, but you are a great pitcher. God made you to be that, too, and that means you are a celebrity, part of a world where I don't belong."

His fingers tightened. "We belong together," he said, a fierce light shining in his face. "Maybe we won't be together every minute because you're going to get that teaching job someday and I'm going to play ball, but that doesn't matter."

"Are you sure?"

He nodded. "I was wrong when I said my home was where the mound is." He put his hands on her face, long fingers stroking her cheeks. "My home is where you are."

She pressed her lips together to stop them trembling.

"Do you love me, Gina?" he said. "Just me, Cal Crawford, and his sad sack dog, not the guy who throws a ball for a living?"

Did she love him? Was it right? The tingle started in her heart and spread to her whole body, warming a path through her with light and love. Trickles of delight flashed through her memory — the ranch, beep ball, washing dishes, sitting on the floor of his San Francisco house, their road trips, windows open, hair flying, Tippy between them.

"Yes, Cal. I do love you, more than any man I've ever known."

His face lit up with a grin that erased the care and worry from his eyes, kindling them with joy. "Will you marry me, Gina Palmer?"

Brimming with wild delight, she nodded, and he pulled her in for a kiss. Their lips joined in a perfect union, warm, loving, filled with promise for the future. How perfect, how right. Gina's heart overflowed with pleasure.

Tippy yipped twice.

"But not tonight," she suddenly shrieked, shoving him to the door. "You've got forty minutes to make it to the airport."

"Too late," he said, still looking at her through that hazy grin. "I'll have to catch a later flight. Someone else will start on opening day."

"Oh no they won't," Gina said, scooping up her purse in one hand and Tippy in the other.

"We aren't going to make it to the airport in forty minutes," he said.

"Not if you're driving," she said, "and it's thirty-nine minutes." She shoved him to the door, propelling him down the stairs.

What followed was a harrowing drive during which she heard Cal gulp hard and struggle for breath as she wove in and out of traffic. They made it to the security checkpoint after the team had already been cleared. The guys stood on the other side, staring in openmouthed astonishment as Cal whirled Gina in his arms, pink curlers flying. Tippy pranced around their ankles.

"I wish you would fly out with me," Cal said.

"Tippy and I will drive. It's much safer than flying."

"With you at the wheel, I'm not so sure," he said with a chuckle.

Aggie cupped his hands to his mouth. "Hey, Boots. What's going on?"

"Gina and I are going to be married," Cal called back.

There was a hearty cheer from the players.

" 'Bout time, Boots," Ag hollered. "You finally made the winning pitch."

"Yes," Cal said, rubbing Tippy's head and giving Gina another kiss, "I finally did."

Excerpt from *The Falcons' Nest,* an online sports blog by Tom Peterson:

The Falcons sizzled in their season opener thanks to ace pitcher, Cal Crawford. Crawford struck out five in six innings, allowing only five hits and one run with three walks. "Everything just felt right," Crawford said. With his father in the stands, his family and fiancée, Gina Palmer, holding unofficial team mascot Tippy the dog, Crawford led the team to their first season victory. The news has been abuzz since the abduction of the dog by the Falcons' disgruntled team mascot and the discovery of Tippy's whereabouts by this fortunate blogger. Did Tippy's dramatic return fuel Crawford's masterful outing? Pitching Coach Pete Crouchley answered with a shrug and a smile, "There's just something about Tippy."

ABOUT THE AUTHOR

Dana Mentink lives in California, where the weather is golden and the cheese is divine. Dana is a two-time American Christian Fiction Writers Book of the Year winner for romantic suspense and an award winner in the Pacific Northwest Writers Literary Contest. Her suspense novel, *Betrayal in the Badlands,* earned a Romantic Times Reviewer's Choice Award. Besides writing, she busies herself teaching third and fourth grade. Mostly, she loves to be home with her husband, two daughters, a dog with social anxiety problems, a chubby box turtle, and a feisty parakeet. Visit her on the web at www.danamentink.com.

To learn more about books by
Dana Mentink
or to read sample chapters,
log on to our
website:**www.harvesthousepublishers.com**